THE ART OF BURGLARY

a short story collection

Happy Birthday Ruth

Joan Baie

Title: The Art of Burglary
Subtitle: a short story collection
Author: Baril, Joan M., 1935-
Subject1: FIC044000 FICTION / Women
Subject2: FIC029000 FICTION / Short Stories
ISBN: 978-1-988829-29-6 (print)
ISBN: 978-1-988829-30-2 (large print)

THE ART OF BURGLARY
a short story collection

All rights reserved. No part of this book may be used or reproduced in any manner whatsoever without prior written permission, except in the case of brief quotations embodied in reviews.

Cover & interior design: Brenda Fisk
First edition © 2024 Joan M. Baril

© 2024 Mischievous Books
MischievousBooks.com
Published in Canada

DEDICATION

To Phil, who told the best stories.

CONTENTS

Acknowledgments i

The Big Hole 1

The Origin of Love..20

The German Spy 26

The Elements of 1950 40

Wine 47

Grace Street..57

The Art of Burglary 70

The Lover 80

The Sisterhood..96

The Rules of Revenge 1952 109

Mr. John Ellis 123

Still Life with Baby...127

Can't See a Cloud in the Sky 137

The Yegg Boy 153

Memories of A Cajun Night...............................178

Horses on the Rio Grande 182

A Ceremony to Initiate a Sweat Lodge 191

The Most Beautiful Breasts in Thunder Bay....196

Dangerous Liaisons...208

About the Author...215

ACKNOWLEDGMENTS

Thank you to the Wabi Sabi Book Club,
The Kaministiquia Writing Group, The Guild,
LUNA (Lakehead Unfinished Novel Association,)
The No Stress Book Club, Margaret Rose
Cunningham, Laura Atkinson, Ulrich Wendt,
Charlie Wilkins, Keith Nymark, Elle Andra Warner,
The Thunder Bay Field Naturalists.

The author wishes to thank
the Ontario Arts Council and the
Government of Ontario for their support.

PART ONE

THE BIG HOLE

"What the hell?" my father said. "Those little guys are still digging that hole." My dad, in his police uniform, had just arrived home from his shift and joined my mother, my sister, and me at our kitchen window, which gave a good view of the yard next door.

We all stared at the big hole, roughly coffin-shaped but much larger and deeper. Even though it was raining lightly, the two neighbouring kids had been at it for hours. Eight-year-old Andrew (Popcorn) Marrin, a square, muscular red-head, knelt on the edge, hoisting up a bucket of soil with the aid of a rope. After trotting a few feet to the end of the lawn, Popcorn, with a casual underhand toss, shot the contents onto a small mountain of dirt that had been growing ever larger as the summer progressed.

Over the twin poles of a ladder scrambled ten-year-old Robert (Rocky) Marrin, covered in dirt from head to runners. Like his younger brother, he was built like a boxer and just as strong. He motioned with his thumb for Popcorn to take his place in the hole and in a few seconds the bucket sequence recommenced.

JOAN BARIL

"One of these days," my sister said, "the sides of that hole are going to collapse and those kids are going to be buried." Her voice held a happy note of anticipation, which she could not suppress. When my father glared at her, she changed her tone. "Why doesn't their mother stop them? Isn't that a parent's responsibility, the safety of the little ones?"

My father frowned. "I did have a word with Elizabeth," he said, "and she told me that children need the creative benefits of imaginative outdoor play for proper intellectual and physical development." He paused. "Whatever the hell that means."

Our neighbour, Elizabeth Marrin, had been a child psychologist who believed in giving children absolute freedom, unencumbered by rules. She explained this to me many times when I went there to babysit. I could only nod, but I wondered how she could ignore the boys' wild behaviour while at the same time imposing strange house rules including a strict vegetarian diet.

My mother shook her head. "She's a lovely, bonnie lassie," she said, "and as soft-headed as yesterday's haggis. Too bad the father's not around to set those wee imps straight. As for this digging mania, something set them off, I'll be bound. They've been at it every day for a month."

I winced. I knew the purpose of the big hole. The boys were preparing a grave for their father, if he ever showed up. They were convinced he was a vampire and were working on a plan to bury him with a stake through his heart. Unfortunately, I was responsible for the idea. Inadvertently, I had

2

started the scheme in motion and now I didn't know how to stop it.

I was just about to confess, when my mother turned to me. "Janet, ye'll have to babysit those lads tonight."

"Why me?" I cried. "Why always me? Why not Leanna for a change? No! I won't do it!" I was sixteen years old and too big, I thought, to be ordered around like a child, but, even as I protested, I knew the outcome. There was no standing against my mother.

"Don't blether," my mother said. "You know Mrs. Marrin wants you. Not Leanna. She likes you. She pays well. She doesn't want your sister ever since she locked the boys in the hall closet. You'll go and that's it and we'll hear no more about it."

"Nyah, nyah," my sister said, making a horrible face at me and sticking out her tongue. "Putting those brats in the closet was the best thing I ever did."

My sister's first babysitting job had not gone well. It took place last winter a few days after Elizabeth Marrin and her children moved into the small house next door. Rocky and Popcorn had pelted Leanna with Lego, leaped at her from the furniture and tried to tie her feet together. When she tried to restrain them, Popcorn bit her on the neck. That was when she lost her temper and, no weakling herself, grabbed each child by his upper arm, dragged them to the hall closet and threw them in. She put a chair under the doorknob to hold it in place. An hour later, mother Elizabeth arrived and was appalled. She released her pounding, screaming sons and cuddled them to her as she rounded on my sister, who did not hang around. Instead, she shot out the door for home.

Ever since, I was the babysitter of choice.

I always prepared well for my babysitting stints. When I arrived, the boys threw themselves on me, smiling and hugging. As soon as their mother was out the door, Popcorn whispered, "Did you bring the candy?"

I nodded.

"And Elvis?"

I nodded again.

"We sure as hell love you, Janet," Rocky said.

"Yes, we do," Popcorn said. "We hate your sister. She locked us in the closet. Mom says we got a big trauma."

"We did," Rocky explained. "A big one. If you get traumas, our mom says you get neuroses and your brain is infected and you grow up to be mentally diffident. You walk all bent over with your hands touching the ground." He illustrated by doing the gorilla walk around the room.

"Your mother is so right," I said, glancing out the front window to make sure Elizabeth Marrin's blue Datsun was gone. "First Elvis," I said, "and remember, Elvis is worth three candies and if there's any messing up the room you lose two." I took the box of Smarties out of my pocket and held it on high. The boys' wide eyes followed the box as I shook it in the air. Their mother did not allow candy or sweets of any sort. A few Smarties brought them to heel brilliantly.

THE ART OF BURGLARY

My 8-track tape player, hidden in my big purse, was useful because Elizabeth Marrin banned rock and roll from the house. TV was also forbidden, but, as yet, I hadn't thought of a way to smuggle in my family's set. As I set up the tape player and put in the Elvis cassette, the boys were jiggling with excitement. At the first guitar chords, they began to dance wildly, waving their arms. "Hound dog!" they yelled. "Hound dog!" The house shook, but I stood ready to prevent any damage. In the middle of an aerial somersault, Popcorn's arm hit the standing lamp. I grabbed it just in time.

"Two candies off," I yelled.

"No-o-o," Popcorn wailed and threw himself on the chesterfield. But he knew I would not relent. Once, during a previous babysitting occasion, the boy, angered by the penalty, threw himself on me and bit my arm. Even as I felt his sharp teeth sink into the area above my wrist, I managed to grab him and slam him into a chair. Holding him in place by the shoulders and avoiding the kicking legs, I explained that, if he ever bit me again I would tell my father, who was a policeman, and he would go to jail. That was the end of the biting.

So far.

But I was always on my guard.

Both Popcorn and Rocky had met the police before, although not my father directly. A few weeks after they arrived in Port Arthur, they had emptied out all the gas from the gas pump in the yard of the Ontario Ministry of Natural Resources at the end of our street. They also released the pedigree poodle in the next block from its cage, put there because it was in heat. The dog was lost for two days. Each time they'd been let off with a warning. Recently, a rumour was going around that they picked up cigarette butts, removed the tobacco, put it in an old pipe, and collected five cents for five puffs from the kids in the neighbourhood. When I questioned them, they denied it strenuously.

The Elvis tape ended and the two collapsed on the rug. I doled out the Smarties, three for Rocky and only one for Popcorn. I did not allow a choice of colours. The boys regarded the candies gravely as if they were precious gems, turning them over, admiring them and, after slowly licking the hard coating, compared the colours of their tongues. I found this disgusting, but I let them do it because it kept them quiet. Then they had to wash their hands and faces, brush their teeth, and put on their pyjamas. These tasks were worth two Smarties each and were done quickly.

They snuggled down beside me on the couch ready for their comic book and goodnight story. Little drops of water clung to their fuzzy red brush-cut heads. Their smiles were wide and innocent. They smelled of soap, toothpaste, and Smarties. Their hard square bodies leaned against me as they regarded the new comic with happy anticipation.

"Superman today," I said, as I unrolled the magazine and showed them the cover. Comics were forbidden in the Marrin household, so both boys stayed close as I read the entire thing through. Because they sat quietly without

THE ART OF BURGLARY

roughhousing, kicking me or punching, they each earned their reward of two Smarties.

"Time for bed. But first your bedtime story."

It was at this stage, during my first session as a babysitter last winter that I made my big mistake. I had planned to tell stories from Canadian history, to give them at least something of value. So I'd said, "I'll tell you the story of Laura Secord."

"We know Laura Secord," Popcorn had said. "Her picture's in the school. She had a stupid cow."

"She saved Canada," I said.

"Boring," said Rocky. "Why did she take the cow with her anyway?" He slipped off the couch to go who knew where.

"But," I said, thinking fast, "What you don't know is that Laura Secord was a vampire."

"A what?" he said. He climbed back up beside me.

"Yes," I said, quickly explaining what a vampire was. I described Laura's pointed teeth, her staring eyes, her lust for blood. I explained that she stayed in the cabin all day because one beam of sunlight would kill her. That was why she did not run away when the American soldiers came. But when night arrived, she said she had to milk the cow. Then, she took the animal with her on her sixteen-mile-trek so she could drink its blood.

The boys nodded. It all made sense to them.

I spun out the story as long as possible, heading for the big finish when Laura reached the Canadian troops before the sun came up, delivered her message and ran off to spend the day in a cave. I described the next night when she went back to

JOAN BARIL

the cabin and released her husband, who was also a vampire. The couple pounced on the American soldiers who had fallen asleep. Later they threw the desiccated bodies into the Niagara River where they went over the falls and were never seen again.

Popcorn and Rocky were so enthralled, I hated to break the spell. I added the little known fact that Laura and her husband, now heroes, lived on for many years until the villagers discovered they were vampires and killed them. I described in detail how the angry neighbours ran stakes through their hearts and buried them in a deep coffin-shaped grave.

"That was one hell of a great story," said Rocky, accepting his candy reward. That night, as I walked them into their shared bedroom, I felt bad for filling their innocent minds with such tripe.

"We had one damn big trauma today," Rocky said as he climbed into bed. "The biggest."

"What?" I said.

"Our father is coming back to live with us. We don't like him. He has a giant neurosis."

"He gives me traumas," Popcorn said. "I'll grow up an idiot. Or maybe a moron." He jumped up and started to punch the quilted headboard of his bed. "Pow! Pow!" I let him punch because the thing was in shreds anyway.

"When's he coming?" I said.

"We don't know," Rocky said. "Mom doesn't know a damn thing."

"Who told you he was coming?"

"Some big kids up the street."

"Do you believe that?"

"Damn right," said Rocky. "When we were little he always came back until Mom made him go away again."

As I tucked them in and counted out two Smarties each to eat in bed, I assured them that the big kids were playing a joke, but they looked skeptical. They could now read for half an hour in bed before I turned out the light. Their mother had started this practice and I continued it with one difference. The half-hour read was worth five Smarties, but any roughhousing and all would be forfeit. As I closed the bedroom door, I heard them whispering excitedly to each other. When I came back thirty minutes later, Rocky said, "We've got it figured out. Our dad is a vampire."

"What? I don't get it. That's silly. It's just a story." I doled out the last candies.

Just before I turned off the light, I heard Rocky say to his brother, "Don't worry, Popcorn. We'll be ready for him."

I regretted that story then and regretted it more later when I saw them digging the hole and guessed what was in their minds. I did nothing, because weeks went by and the absent dad never showed up. The gossip at Port Arthur Collegiate claimed Elizabeth Marrin had separated from her husband, returning to live in her hometown. Her rich father, who owned a lumber company, bought her the house and paid her a generous allowance. No one knew why her marriage broke up, but I reasoned that Elizabeth, so softhearted and scatty, probably put up with a lot before she left him. I believed it was unlikely that he would ever turn up in Port Arthur, not with her powerful father around.

My more immediate problem, I felt, was I had hooked them on gore. After the Laura Secord session, they demanded more Canadian history. With the help of the horror comics sold at the corner store, I was able to think up a variety of plots: David (Frankenstein) Thompson; Prime Minister Mackenzie Zombie King; Suzanna Moodie, Werewolf of the Bush and so on.

"The story tonight is about John A. Macdonald," I said, settling back on the chesterfield.

"Canada's first prime minister," Rocky said. "We studied him in school. Our father said he was a drunk."

"Yes," I said, "The reason is this: he was dead. He was one of the living dead. Under his clothes, his body was all green and hung down in shreds. He only drank alcohol to stay in the land of the living."

The boys nodded their understanding and the story was on.

Late the next afternoon, I hurried home after choir practice to see a large station wagon in front of the Marrin house. It was parked on the small front lawn taking up most of the space. It looked more like a candidate for the wrecking yard than a workable vehicle. One of the tires was almost flat, creating a severe sideways lean. The chrome was spotted and twisted, and in a few places missing entirely, as if someone had hacked off chunks. Deep scratches crisscrossed the wooden sides, which were dark with dirt. Rust had eaten the metal all around the wheels and the bottom of the doors, and spattered dark red spots across the hood.

I wanted to peek inside the vehicle, but I did not dare. Someone, maybe the returned father and husband, for the car must be his, could be watching from the house. As I walked slowly past, I noted the back bumper was held in place with rusted wire. A blackened exhaust hung underneath, almost touching the ground. The back window was covered in either black paint or paper; I could not discern which. This vehicle was so ugly it would give anyone a trauma, I thought, with a pang for the boys. Their friends would tease them unmercifully.

"So, the missing husband turned up," my mother said, as she was ladling out the barley soup. A large macaroni and cheese casserole sat on top of the stove. "Your dad's late. He's in court. We'll eat with him later. Your sister's at volleyball practice. So stoke yersel' up on soup and we'll have a late meal." She sat down at the table, a cup of tea in front of her.

"Did you see him?" I asked.

"Indeed, I did. He walked in as if he owned the place and later carried in a few boxes. I guess he's here to stay. He's nay bargain, that one. Braw looking lassie like Elizabeth sure picked a dud. Peaked little feller. Face as dour as a burnt boot. Still an all, he may keep those wee devils in line."

"How'd she meet him?" I was interested in Elizabeth's story.

"She told me once," my mother said, saucering her tea and blowing on it to cool it, "that she met him at a party when she was at university in Toronto."

"If he was so poor," I said, thinking of the station wagon, "and so bad looking, why marry him?"

My mother gave me a long strange look. "Well, I'll tell you something, Janet. A bonny rich lass attracts a certain type. The predator. I think she had to marry him after a while. At least that's what she hinted. She only said her parents insisted."

I was amazed. My mother had never talked like this before, as if I were a grown-up. "You mean," I said, "she got... pregnant?"

"Aye," my mother said. "I dinna know for sure but..." She let the rest of the sentence hang.

An unpleasant thought hit me. "Do you think he got her pregnant on purpose so she had to marry him? To get at her money?"

"Possible," my mother said. "It's been done before."

"But what made her leave him?"

"Ah, on that subject she said naught. It could be anything. Let this be a lesson, Janet. It's a hard life for a woman if she's nae canny when chosin' a husband."

During the next week, I caught only a few glimpses of Mr. Marrin. The digging in the back yard went on as usual. On Thursday, to my surprise, Elizabeth Marrin phoned and asked if I would babysit next Saturday afternoon. When I arrived, the husband was sitting at the wheel of Elizabeth's Datsun and, as soon as I got inside the house, he honked the horn and kept it up. Elizabeth, flustered, grabbed purse, rain jacket and

12

rain hat. "I made some seaweed snacks in case we're late for dinner," she said. "And Janet, it looks like rain. If it does, will you get the washing off the line?"

I nodded.

I suggested to the boys we go to the park and they agreed. Leaving by the back door, we walked down the lane that ran beside the house toward busy Arthur Street and Waverley Park. Predictably, once there, the brothers went wild, wrestling like bear cubs on the grass, vaulting over the ornamental cannons, somersaulting down the hills and chasing each other around the war memorial. We circled my high school, where they became absorbed in hunting for pieces of chalk thrown out the windows by unruly students on the last day of school. Recalling the horrible seaweed snacks waiting in the fridge, I took them down the hill to Peanut Jim's Confectionary for a Persian donut and a coke.

They were in sugar bliss on the return journey, so I felt it was a good time to ask questions. "How's life with your dad?"

"Trauma," said Popcorn. "We get lots. He hurts me." He pouted, kicked his feet, and punched the air.

"What does he do?" I asked, my heart pounding with fear that I would hear about beatings.

"He does this." Popcorn bent his middle finger with his thumb, flicking it forward on his head. It made a loud snapping sound.

"Yeah," said Rocky, "the bugger flicks us. When we come out of the bathtub, he flicks us with the towel if we start horsing around. And he calls us names and says bad things."

"Such as?"

"Space Aliens. Creatures from the Black Lagoon. Spawn of the Devil. He says we'll end up living in a tarpaper shack on the Nipigon Highway."

"That is not nice," said Popcorn. "It gives me trauma. Besides, he's a vampire."

"Come on," I said. "That's not funny."

"Oh yeah." Rocky was indignant. "Well, put this in your pipe and smoke it, Janet. He's got cases of blood in the car and more in the pantry. He drinks it all day long. He did the same thing long ago when we were little. Blood, blood, damned blood. All day long. Then he passes out."

We had reached the back door of the house. The washing had turned wild, billowing and dancing on the line, barely held in place by the pegs. A bruised sky glowered over us. I heard a far-off noise that might have been thunder.

In the house, Popcorn opened the pantry door to show me several tall bottles of red liquid on the top shelf.

"I think it's wine," I said. "Just wine." I looked around for the clothes basket and spied it under the kitchen table.

"He passes out," said Rocky. "I think he's in the back of the station wagon right now. I think I saw him crawl in there. He's got blankets there and he drinks blood and passes out. He pisses into an empty blood bottle."

"No, Rocky. He went off with your mother."

THE ART OF BURGLARY

"No, Janet, he didn't. He didn't." Rocky clenched his fists and glowered at me. "He got out of Mom's car and walked away up the street and, when she drove off, I think he came back and climbed into the back of the station wagon."

This was more than absurd. I had to check it out. Just then, the first scatter shot of rain hit the windows.

"Stay here," I said, picking up the clothes basket. "I'll get the washing in and then we can talk about this."

The wind, now much stronger, slammed the back door behind me but not before I heard Rocky say, "Come on, Popcorn."

A summer storm in Northern Ontario is fierce and fast. I could feel the temperature dropping as the storm gathered itself over the city, setting the trees in motion and the clothes flailing. I was halfway finished, rushing, not stopping to fold anything, throwing the pins wildly into the basket, as the rain tried to tear the garments from my hands when I heard the roaring, but, this time, it was not thunder. I looked behind me. The station wagon was coming down the lane, black smoke belching from its rear end. Only Rocky's eyes and bullet head showed through the steering wheel as he tried to turn the wagon. It skimmed the first clothesline pole and the platform where I was standing. A loud, unsteady clatter rose from the vehicle as Rocky cranked the wheel. I had a brief glimpse of his square white face as the station wagon slithered across the back lawn, one wheel hitting the edge of the hole and then it fell in with a

15

crash, as if the monstrous thing had fallen apart, leaving only the crunch of broken glass and the screaming inside.

My father was out of our house, running in big leaps. The station wagon was half in and half out, its back end sticking straight up in the air. It was canted on one side without enough room to fall over. Popcorn had cranked down his window and my father, with one foot on the side of the wagon to avoid the spinning tires, leaned forward and yanked him out. Rocky followed. Both were wailing. Blood was running down their faces. Their clothes were awash in red liquid. I could hear sirens converging on us. Later I learned my mother had phoned the ambulance and both the fire and police departments.

I yelled at my father. "Mr. Marrin. He may be in there."

The back door of the wagon popped open. A strange man hung above us for a second and then jumped, toppled over, gathered himself upright and scurried for the house. My dad, in two bounds, had him by the lower arm and was bending him backwards. My mother appeared, snatched up Popcorn, lifted him over her shoulder, and ran with him to our place. I grabbed Rocky and dragged him after her, but the ambulance guy stopped me and took him. My mother handed over Popcorn. She then pushed me toward our house.

"Are you hurt, Janet?" she said once we were inside.

"No. Just wet."

THE ART OF BURGLARY

"Good, put the kettle on then. Keep the door closed. The reporters will be here and we don't want our name in the paper. Why did you leave those brats alone?"

I was stunned. Was I going to be held responsible for the entire fiasco? "I told Mrs. Marrin I would get the washing in." I felt a depressing drop in my stomach as I realized my mother would blame me unjustly. Surprisingly, she said only, "We'el, that's the end of it then. Nae doubt you knew what you were doin'. A nice cup of tea will do us both good and we can watch from the kitchen window."

A week later, my dad explained. "Ronny Marrin was well known in Toronto for making and bootlegging red wine. Things were getting hot so he closed shop, bought the station wagon, loaded it up with the stock and headed north probably selling the goods as he went. Arrived here. We ferreted out a few of his local customers. After a little encouragement, they decided they'd testify for the Crown. So Mr. Marrin is charged with illegal selling of alcohol. Now, he's sitting behind the pipes at the Cooke Street Station. Can't make bail. As it is, he'll not get much. A month or two. You'll see him back next door one of these fine days."

"I doubt it, Duncan," said my mother. "The old man will pay him to get going. Poor Elizabeth'll have no luck getting a divorce, unlucky creature."

"As I was saying," my father said evenly. "He may show up again. Every time he needs money."

17

"The boys will get older and bigger," I said. "They may not get off with a few scrapes and cuts next time," I said. "And neither will he."

Both parents looked at me. They were frowning and nodding, as if they were considering my words. "Very good, Janet," my father said. "Those lads are a force of nature, right enough. You may be right. This story is not over, not by a long shot."

But we were wrong. On Monday, Elizabeth Marrin's father showed up with a crew of lumberyard workers. By late afternoon, the station wagon was gone and the hole filled. Ronny Marrin spent only six weeks in jail. According to my dad, the old man met him outside, handed him a few bucks and told him to hit the trail. He never did return, as we all expected.

Both boys, superficially cut and bruised, seemed unaffected by their experience. I continued to babysit from time to time for the next two years. As they got older, they became quieter, as if their excess energy had drained into the big hole along with the station wagon. Surprisingly, Elizabeth got her divorce, married again, and moved to Winnipeg. We lost track of the family completely. Years later, I heard both brothers had been brilliant high school students and star football players. Later still, I learned Popcorn became an engineer and Rocky had started a branch of his grandfather's lumber business in Kenora. They both married, had children.

"That accident traumatized those kids, teaching them a much needed lesson, which made them see the error of their wild ways," my sister said. This

THE ART OF BURGLARY

was her favourite theory, which she repeated every time the subject of the Marrin family came up.

But I had my own idea. Maybe Mr. Marrin was a sort of vampire, who in Toronto, attempted to suck the life force out of Elizabeth and her children, turning up drunk and unpleasant until she gave him money. Had he repeated the performance many times until she fled? Did he have the same plan in mind when he showed up again in Port Arthur? If this was the case, the brothers had done a good day's work. Even though they were very young at the time, I believe they understood this very well.

THE ORIGIN OF LOVE

First and foremost, Evadne.

Evadne was six years old and I was four. It seemed to me that she had always been there, always watching from her yard across the street for me to come outside. Then she would take her little brother, Sonny, by the hand, explain they were crossing the road and over they came. Only occasionally did I have to go across and call on her.

In my mind's eye, I see two little girls and a toddler playing at earth level, picking up stones to build things or looking for pretty leaves or pieces of glass to put in our imaginary houses hidden under back stoops and the front steps of neighbours, or among trees or behind bushes. We moved through the property of contingent neighbours as if it were our own, but we moved stealthily. I still believe that few of the residents noticed the three ragged urchins crouching between the lilac bush and the basement wall, or hunkered in the raspberry patch, or behind the shed or the garage. These crevices and play spaces were very important to us, and we loved them, and felt an urge to protect them for ourselves. It was second nature to us to be wary and avoid the adults who might very well tell us to get out of their yard and not come back.

THE ART OF BURGLARY

Of course, we also played out in the open, sometimes in my back yard, with its stone wall and huge crab apple tree, or in the back lanes and the vacant lots, still scattered here and there so close to the centre of town.

Evadne was the leader and the centre. From her flowed incredible warmth and caring which I can feel even now, so far and so long does love travel. She brushed the sticks out of my hair, she picked me up if I fell, she waited for me when we crawled through the blackberries, she held my hand when we crossed a wall. She did the same for Sonny, who seldom spoke but followed us dumbly and happily, very dirty of face and clothes.

Even now, sixty-five years later, I can still, rather dimly, see her face. It was a wide brown face with a square jaw, a strong straight smile, her forehead fringed with thick black bangs. She was a sturdy child, strong and well-coordinated. She could climb the crab apple tree and easily pull up Sonny, who was as sturdy as she, and then reach down and lift me up under the arms as if I were an apple leaf. She would jump down and edge us, one at a time, along the low heavy bough until we were well hidden in the tangle at the end.

I never remember her cuddling or kissing me—my parents never did either, nor as a young child did I expect them to do so. Still, I knew, knew in my bones, Evadne loved me, just as I also knew deep within the same bones, that my parents did not.

One morning in September when I was five years old, Evadne crossed the road without Sonny, an unusual occurrence. She was unusually neat and wore a clean dress. She told me she could not play that day because she had to go to school. I followed her down the hill to Algoma Street and over to the traffic lights on the corner of Arthur Street. I was not lost—the Baptist Church where I went to Sunday school was on this corner. When she started to cross at the lights, heading downtown to St. Andrew's School, I knew I dared not follow her. I felt I had already come quite far from home. As I started to cry, she told me over and over she would come back and off she went.

I sat down on the roadside curb to wait. I felt the world had stopped somehow. When a policeman came and told me to go home, I howled all the way up the hill.

Eventually I would lose Evadne forever but not yet.

Evadne's house, across the street from mine, was a very poor place indeed, an unpainted small two-storey structure surrounded by a dirt lot. It stood in sharp contrast to the older and deeply landscaped houses around it. I have no idea when Evadne's house was built. It had been a "shack" for a long time, a place without siding and with a rickety wooden stoop at the front door. But it was not the only shack in town.

In those years, after the long Depression, the city was dotted with homemade houses, often very small. My friend Bobby Clark lived with his large family in a three-room slant-roof insul-brick house around the corner on Jean Street. Roy Sykes, another friend, lived down a lane off Regent Street in a ramshackle two-storey that had not been

THE ART OF BURGLARY

painted or repaired for many years. This house was in such bad condition that the snow came through cracks in the walls. Therefore, although Evadne's shacky house was alone in our block, it was not alone in the neighbourhood.

I seldom crossed the street to call for Evadne and, when I did, I was left on the wooden front stoop and never invited inside. Except once. Her cat had had kittens and would I like to see them? Of course! And so I was taken upstairs into a bedroom where five enchanting fat kittens and mama cat lay in a cardboard box in a closet. The kittens, their eyes tight shut, squirmed and waved tiny searching paws. I thought they looked like buds, flower or leaf buds, trying to open to full life.

Naturally, I had the idea that I would like to have one of the kittens for my own and put the suggestion strongly to my mother.

A mistake.

The next day, she came across the road to see them. I remember as I climbed the stairs with her, in some odd sort of way, I was seeing Evadne's house through my mother's eyes and realizing what a funny place it was. The rooms contained little furniture. In the bedroom, a mattress lay on the board floor. No curtains covered the windows. I do not remember if Evadne's mother was present, but I do remember being told, quite sharply, that we would not take a kitten.

The next day, both my mother and father spoke to me at dinner. I was not to play with Evadne anymore. I was not to cross the street. I was not to go to Evadne's house. I was no longer to be friends with Evadne.

I reacted in horror. I was being cut off from the only person who loved me and for what? I remember crying and crying in a terrible welter of heartbreak and confusion. Why had this happened? My tearful questions were not answered. At the same time, I was gripped by an overwhelming fear that Evadne would disappear from my life forever.

Here, I was right. It was the end of summer. I was six years old and ready to start Central School in September. During those last few days, I saw Evadne only a couple of times and we played as usual but far from my house where my mother could not see. A few days after I started school, I came home to be told Evadne's family had moved. As far as I was concerned, Evadne had vanished from the earth. I never saw her or heard of her again.

Some years later, when I was in my teens, I realized that Evadne and her family were Ojibway. I recalled that my mother, who never supervised me when I played outside and, in general, seldom paid attention to me or my activities, or the activities of the neighbourhood, had not realized this fact until the day she had gone across the street to see the kittens. My parents seldom displayed their prejudice, but, when I was a teen, I knew it lurked. At last, I understood why the friendship had been forbidden.

Evadne planted inside me a golden seed, a tiny glowing speck of love that I can still feel today. Such a seed creates the feeling, the belief, strong as

THE ART OF BURGLARY

a rock, that someone loves you and that this love can never change. I believe now, without Evadne, I would have been lost, just as the unloved child is always, in a certain and important sense, lost in the world.

I owe that little girl more than I can say.

THE GERMAN SPY

When Charlotte and I walked down the hill to the Modern Funeral Parlour, we held hands because we were scared. We were going to the funeral of our playmate, Lorraine, who we called Rainy. Charlotte's twin brother, Artie, who sometimes played with Rainy, trailed after us.

"I don't know, Janet. I don't know," Charlotte kept saying. She was trying to find enough courage to look at Rainy in her coffin, to see her dead.

I squeezed her hand. "Remember we haven't seen her for a while, so she'll look different. Dead people always do." I thought of my grandmother who looked like a sweet old lady in her casket, but, in real life, was a very frightening person.

Rainy and her parents were new people brought into Port Arthur by the war, strangers related to no one. They lived in a suite, unlike most families in Port Arthur, who lived in houses. When Rainy went to the hospital, which happened often, we were never taken to visit. When we heard she'd died, we begged our mothers to let us go to the funeral. That may have been a mistake. I could see that now.

"Thank heavens Rainy never told anyone about what we did to the German spy," I whispered.

THE ART OF BURGLARY

"Maybe she never figured it out," said Charlotte. "She always was a bit dozy."

❖

"Get up here, Rainy!" my sister called. "A German spy is getting out of a car behind your house." My sister was up in the loft of the old stable. I was down on the main floor guiding Rainy's feet up the ladder.

Even though Rainy was thirteen, four years older than I, she was clumsy and scared. I had to place her feet on the rungs and tell her over and over that she could do it. My sister, who was six, had gone up without using her feet, swinging like a monkey.

That morning, the radio said Canada was infested with German spies. They lurked everywhere, sabotaging our war effort. It seemed logical to me that if there were German spies everywhere, then there must be at least one in Port Arthur.

"A car!" Rainy said. "Very suspicious." Because of the war, most of the neighbourhood cars were up on blocks. This included the Packard below us in the garage section of the old stable. In the entire neighbourhood, only Doctor Gordon had gas coupons.

The stable was a holdover from the long ago horse and buggy days. It stood in a brushy back corner of the neighbour's lot. The downstairs consisted of the garage on one side and a room of horse stalls on the other. Old boards, broken

27

screen windows and paint cans filled the horse area. Upstairs was the airy open loft, probably once a hayloft. It was a favourite place to play.

Through the cracked panes, we could look down on the back parking area of Rainy's place. A strange man walked around the car and leaned into the passenger window talking to someone, and then, every once in a while, he straightened up and looked about in a very suspicious manner. Once, he stared directly at our window.

We froze in terror.

Eventually, and slowly, the spy turned back to the car. We let out our breath.

Aside from the fact that he had a car when hardly anyone else did, he was dressed in a peculiar way, as if he had just come from the woods, even though it was late September. He was wearing jeans and a sloppy sweater and, also unusual, no hat or cap. "Perhaps he's been hiding out in the forest," I whispered.

He was a tall, skinny guy with a fierce snappy voice going a mile a minute. Then, in a quick change of tone, he laughed loudly, opened the passenger door and a woman came out.

"Ah ha!" Rainy said. "His accomplice. All spies have them."

He reached into the back seat and took out a square black case and placed it on the ground.

"His radio," whispered Rainy.

He then walked around to the trunk, opened it and took out another black case and handed it to the woman.

THE ART OF BURGLARY

"Her radio," said Rainy. "They use radios to send messages to Hitler."

I studied the accomplice. She looked familiar even at a distance. Bubsie Reitman! The best friend of my cousin, Midge. She wore the same wine-coloured coat with the fur collar that Bubsie always wore, and she had the same brown hair with a big roll in the front and another across the back. She too was looking around in a very suspicious manner, studying the back windows of the old Trelevyn mansion. The man picked up his radio and they both scurried like mice across the small parking area and into the back door. Through the broken panes, we could hear them laughing.

My sister began to bawl, but Rainy gathered her in with a fat arm. "Don't worry," she whispered. "Those spies can't get us. My dad's in the navy and your dad's a policeman, so we'll all be fine." She put her arm around me too and I could feel the squashiness of her big stomach and the smell of her Hollywood soap.

I put my hand up to stroke her silky hair. "I love you, Rainy," I said.

"I love you too, Janet," she said.

The next day, at recess, Rainy came over from the big girls' section of the playground where she usually just stood around because none of the big girls would play with her. "He's living on the second floor," she said, "in the little apartment across the landing from us. After school, I'll show you and you can break in, and check the place out."

I stepped back. "What? Break in? Why me?"

29

"It's your duty, Janet." Rainy was severe. "The grown-ups will never believe us. So it's up to you to save Canada."

Rainy's apartment was in a three-storey mansion, built by Mr. Trelevyn, who we called the famous Silver Magnate, because he owned so many silver mines. The whole Trelevyn family was dead and the place had been turned into suites, a novelty in our town.

No one was in the front entry when we arrived. I followed Rainy as she huffed up the carpeted stairs, past the window seat in the curve where we stopped to take a look at the parking lot—no spy car—and then to the second floor landing. We didn't have to worry about Rainy's parents. Her father was hardly ever home and neither was her mother who, strangely enough, had a job. She worked at the Royal Canadian Naval Base, where, according to Rainy, she spent every day doing puzzles.

"Over here," Rainy said pointing to a varnished door with the number 4 scrawled on it in red paint. "First, we have to check out the back stairs."

This dark and scary staircase ran down behind a narrow door set in the corner of the landing. In the old days of the Silver Magnate, it was used by servants. I opened the door and looked far down into the shadows. No one. Then I tried the spy's door. Locked.

"No problem," Rainy said, "you can get in by the dumbwaiter."

"What?"

THE ART OF BURGLARY

"Look," said Rainy and lifted a small square panel set halfway up the wall at the top of the service stairs. "The Silver Magnate built this tunnel down through the wall, so they could hoist up trays and stuff from the kitchen and take the dirty dishes down. So the Magnate could have his breakfast in bed."

I leaned over and saw a deep well, a dark chute heading down into blackness. Directly across, another panel, partly raised, must open into the spy's suite, but it was too far to reach. "We just lift that door over there and then," Rainy said. "You can jump across."

Impossible. I would fall into the hole and I knew it. Even my sister wouldn't be able to get across. "Where's the thing-a-ma-bob that lifted the trays?" I said, still staring into the dark below.

"It hasn't worked for years," said Rainy. "However, I have complete confidence in you, Janet."

Before I could argue with her, we heard a noise from the bottom of the servants' stairs, the sound of the back door opening. A shaft of light suddenly appeared on the lower wall and a voice, a man's voice, said impatiently, "Hurry up."

We backed across the landing. Rainy was heading for her own front door until I grabbed her by the arm and pulled her up the staircase that led to the third floor. There, around the turn, we could sit and be hidden.

"This case is awful heavy," said a woman's voice that I recognized as Bubsie's.

31

"Well, I can't leave them in the car, can I?" said the spy.

We heard her slam the case down. "Here you go, Karl. You take it."

Karl? Obviously a German name. We looked at each other with rounded eyes and, at that moment, I started to believe in my own imagination. He really must be a spy, I thought, and not just part of a game.

"Don't bang it down like that." His voice was sharp. "I have a lot invested in there."

"Fine, fine," Bubsie said.

"These back stairs are the best feature of this dump." He started singing softly. "I got those back stairs blues..." His feet made a tapping sound as if he were dancing. "I'm a back stairs man. Oh mama, you know what I want and this backstairs man is comin' for ya."

"Oh, for crying in the sink," Bubsie said.

"What the hell's with you now?"

"I just remembered what I forgot," Bubsie said. "To say good-bye. So," she said in a sing-song voice, "Bye, bye, kiddo." And we heard her steps turn and clatter down and down. The outside door at the bottom banged.

"Stupid damn broad," said the spy. "Dumb dame." We heard his key in the lock.

Rainy and I looked at each other and made big O's with our mouths. We did not like the spy at all. His door slammed.

"Good for her," I said. "She doesn't want to be an accomplice anymore."

THE ART OF BURGLARY

In the month that followed, my best friend, Charlotte, and I kept track of the spy from the window of the old stable. We climbed up there almost every day after school to see him drive in, usually about five o'clock or so. Rainy did not join us; she was in the hospital again, so I'd brought Charlotte into the secret mission. I didn't include my sister—a blabber—and certainly not Charlotte's twin brother, Artie, an altar boy who told his mother everything. The spy came and went, always taking the cases from the car and sometimes a very long bundle wrapped in black cloth.

"A rifle," Charlotte said. "Bet ya anything."

Bubsie never returned, but another woman came often, the new accomplice, and then, surprisingly, a woman from the next block, whose husband was with the army in Italy. "She must really need the money," Charlotte said grimly. "Traitor! I bet she gets a cheque straight from Hitler."

At night in bed, I tried to think how to cross the black hole that was the dumbwaiter and, eventually, an idea occurred to me. I wondered why I'd not thought of it before.

After school the next day, Charlotte and I hastened into the stable to get a good wide board that was not rotten. We found one about the same height as ourselves. Together, we carried it down the lane to the Trelevyn property and up the back stairs and, at the top, leaned it on the wall while I lifted the panel of the dumbwaiter. Together we pushed one end of the board to the far side of the black hole, setting it under the partly-open panel.

We looked at each other. It was suddenly getting hard to breathe, so I knew we had to move fast. "Hold the board," I whispered and climbed on, kneeing my way across, not looking at the darkness below. Carefully I put my hand under the lip of the wooden square and, after it gave a little squeak, it slid up nicely. I wiggled headfirst through the opening and, using my hands, slid slowly and carefully onto the floor.

I jumped up to hold the board for Charlotte and she too moved inch by inch. At the end, I gripped the seat of her jeans as she slid head first to safety.

We had emerged into the spy's living room, a small, dim, high-ceilinged place with no carpet, wood floors and a Venetian blind on the single window. There was a sort of nook on one side, a kitchen area with a sink full of dishes, and an old stove. At the back was a small hall with two doors leading from it. The living room section contained a couch, a tall radio and a strange twisty lamp which stood in the middle of the floor. The place was jammed with cardboard and wooden boxes of various sizes. Obviously, the spy had not unpacked yet.

"Look," I whispered, pointing.

Several round metal cases sat on the kitchen table. They looked like film canisters, familiar items from movie day at school. Each sported a bright white label covered with sprawly handwriting. I picked one up, opened it, and pushing aside the black cloth cover, pulled on a black tab. Dark ribbons of film spewed out and tumbled on the floor at my feet in long spiraling curls. *Ah ha!*

Obviously the spy had been filming Canada's war effort.

I smiled at Charlotte, who picked up another and the same thing happened. The thin film corkscrewed out of the can like a squirrel from its hole and twisted away in a satisfying pattern over the table and on to the floor. I opened a third and then a fourth and watched delighted as the film, black and shiny, sprang from each canister like a snake. The fifth I held over the dumbwaiter to watch the film whistle down and down into the blackness below.

"Is that you, Karl?" A woman's sleepy voice came from somewhere in the back of the suite.

My heart lurched so hard, I felt it might fall out. For a minute, the two of us were frozen in place. Then, we tiptoed over to the door, carefully turned the key in the lock and got out, clicking it behind us. My head was thumping as if drums were playing inside. "The board," I whispered as we crept toward the back stairs. I pulled it towards me and hung on as it twisted in my hands while Charlotte closed the dumb waiter. Then we each took an end and slipped down the stairs as quickly as we could.

Once outside we ditched the board and ran across the tiny parking area, past two cars up on blocks, past an old garage and down the back lane. Charlotte was a swift runner. Not me. I always got stitches in my side. However, I learned an important lesson that day. You can ignore anything if you're scared enough. We finally slumped down in a hidden spot between the old stable and the raspberry bushes.

JOAN BARIL

"She didn't see us. I'm sure she didn't see us." I breathed. "I hope. I hope."

❖

Rainy came out of hospital three months later, just before Christmas. Her mother phoned to ask if I would come and play with her. I found her on the couch in her pyjamas with a Hudson Bay blanket over her knees. She looked older and a lot skinnier, but, as soon as I saw her wide soft smile and her round brown eyes, I was struck once more with the warm rush of love I always felt for her. I jumped on the couch to kneel beside her. I threw my arms around her neck.

"I'm so glad you're better." I nuzzled her silky brown hair.

Her arms, now as knobby as sticks through her pyjama sleeves, pulled me close.

"I'll bring you both a glass of milk," her mother said, pushing a small table in front of us. She opened a box of Laura Secord chocolates and slid them toward me. "Help yourself," she said. It took only a second for me to recover from the surprise of an entire box of candy. I dove in.

Rainy showed me all her treasures, everything fresh from the store: a new Snakes and Ladders game, a new Chinese Checkers, a new pack of cards. Even a new colouring book, "Famous Movie Stars," although it seemed to me that Rainy, at thirteen, should be too old for colouring.

Nevertheless, we chose facing pages and set to, picking our crayons from an enormous new set.

THE ART OF BURGLARY

Not one broken crayon in the lot. As well, the box could be made to stand upon a cunning wooden rack. I'd never seen such an array and it took me ages to choose the colours for Carmen Miranda's Latin costume. Rainy did Rita Hayworth dressed as a gypsy. After we got tired of colouring, we played Clue and then a card game called Backward Rummy.

Darkness comes early on a December afternoon in Northern Ontario. I was bouncing with happiness and full of chocolates, but after a while, I saw the room filling with shadows. Time to go home. We gathered up the cards and I put all the games away in the bookcase. I straightened her blanket and pillows. Rainy's mother came and switched on the lamps.

"Good-bye, good-bye." I struggled into my parka and pulled on my overshoes. Rainy giggled when I blew her big kisses.

"Come back tomorrow," she called.

"Here," said Rainy's mother, handing me the half-full box of chocolates. "Take these."

I flew down the curving staircase and out into the glossy dark heading for the back lane and home, eating chocolates all the way.

The next day, Rainy was back in hospital. It was only then I realized I never told her about the German spy. I never told her of our amazing feat. I never shared my secret glow as girl hero, the nine-year-old who'd saved Canada and probably the entire British Empire.

Rainy never left the hospital. Three months later, she was dead of leukemia.

❖

In the funeral home, Charlotte's brother wouldn't go up to look at Rainy in her casket. He sat in the back pew and folded his arms. Charlotte and I held hands as we ventured down the aisle towards the shiny box set on pedestals. It took a minute to recognize Rainy. She looked like a mummy, a dried up prune girl, her face thin and wrinkly, her hair dull and straight. Only her dark lashes, lying on her cheeks, remained the same. When Charlotte started to blubber, I put my arm around her shoulder and pushed her back to our pew.

Throughout the service, I watched the backs of Rainy's parents, her father in a navy uniform, her mother in a black coat. The chapel echoed with her sobbing. Only a dozen or so grown-ups were present. The funeral wasn't what I'd expected. When some navy guys lifted the coffin, I was filled with a sort of sickness, a hopeless feeling in my stomach that was not comfortable at all.

I often thought of Rainy in the following years. I summoned up the warmth of her loving spirit. It seemed impossible it simply vanished.

And there were so many things I did not know. Had the woman in the bedroom heard us? What was he filming because, by now, seven years after we exposed his film, I no longer believed he was a

German spy. And what did he say when he got home that day?

"The old Trelevyn place is to be torn down." My father came into the kitchen holding his newspaper. He was wearing his police pants and boots, getting ready to go on shift. I was doing my algebra homework at the kitchen table. My mother was making scones.

"Remember that National Film Board guy who lived there during the war? The one with all the visiting ladies?" my father said. "An entire month's work destroyed."

"Sweet revenge," my mother said.

"We never found out which gal did it. They all denied it. In the end, we couldn't lay charges. Those haywire artist fellows..."

"He went back to Toronto," my mother said, "and I say good riddance." She banged the oven door shut.

"We don't need those types in Port Arthur. Not with young girls around."

THE ELEMENTS OF 1950

"I thought it was about sex and now you say it's not?" I was aghast. The film, which was to be shown in the school auditorium that morning, was supposed to answer the question at last. All the girls in the high school would see it in the morning and the boys in the afternoon.

"No," said Alena Charlotte. "It's not about sex. It's about VD."

"What's that?"

"Venereal disease. It is what men get when they go to prostitutes."

We were speaking in low voices as we walked towards the school a block away from our houses. I shot a glance behind us where Alena Charlotte's twin brother, Artie, was walking with his friend Jack. I felt I looked pretty good that morning in my red wool skirt with its cinch belt, my striped batwing-sleeve jersey top, and my black baby doll suede shoes. A metal pendant hung between my pointed Wonder Bra breasts and I was wearing just a touch of Chantilly perfume.

I was in love with Artie—but then, I was in love with almost all the boys in my grade ten class. The boys were paying no attention to us. This was not unusual—they never did. They too were talking in low tones and I felt sure the topic was the same.

"We were at Mrs. Hutchin's last night and this is what she told my mother," Alena Charlotte said. "It's VD only." Mrs. Hutchin was our Latin teacher and a good friend of Alena Charlotte's family.

I was disappointed about the film. What a waste of time. And yet you couldn't argue with Alena Charlotte. Her information was always right. She first told me about prostitutes last year and preposterous as the story was—men paying for sex! Why?

I later learned it was true.

When we were little girls growing up a few houses apart, she had always been the one with the sex information. For instance, in grade six, she found out about menstruation and told me about it. At first, I didn't believe her. You bleed every month and have to wear rags between your legs? Too sick. Whose idea was this anyway?

It turned out she was dead right.

"Don't whine," my mother had said, as she was showing me the harness contraption I had to wear and giving me the standard explanation a Canadian mother always gives to her daughter at this turn in her life: "Even the Queen menstruates."

Oh sure, I thought. Then, rethinking it later, I realized it must be true. Probably Princess Elizabeth and Princess Margaret Rose menstruated as well. Hard as it was to believe, there was a certain reassurance in that fact, a dark secret comfort in thinking about Princess Elizabeth struggling with her harness and dealing with the pads. Royalty, I thought, does serve a purpose after all.

Once, when we were younger kids, playing allies in the Central School yard, Alena Charlotte had blabbed about the penis. I had never heard of the penis before. She must have seen Artie's I suppose, but I had no brothers and had never even seen a naked baby boy. Alena's information cleared up the question that had been on my mind for some time. What exactly was the difference between boys and girls?

My first theory—when I was very little—concerned fingernails. My grandfather and my uncle Everett had each lost the tips of fingers in industrial accidents in the shipyards at Jarrow-on-Tyne in the North of England. Oddly enough, my father had lost the fingertips of one hand in a picture framing factory in Birmingham before he had immigrated to Canada. Thus, when I grew up, all the males around me had few or no fingernails and I assumed—deep thinker that I was—the difference between men and women was simple. The women had all their fingernails and the men did not. It was an explanation that lasted for a few years until I understood that men had a large leaf between their legs.

When I was about eight, my parents bought a set of the *Books of Knowledge*. I studied the photos of Greek and Roman statues and any other depictions of naked men in the art section. Even though I had given up the fingernail theory, I still did not know what a naked boy looked like. I suspected but was not sure they were different. It

42

seemed to me, looking closely at these poor quality reproductions, that the men all had a strange shaped object between their legs that looked very much like a large maple or oak leaf. *Ah ha!* Men grew leaves. No one was going to find me ignorant after this.

Many years later at a party, I had everyone helpless with laughter when I explained the fingernail and maple leaf theories of sexual difference. However, a friend, Pierre, outdid me by stating that, when he was a boy, the same question had puzzled him until he noticed that the men had zip flies in the front of their pants, making it easy to pee, while the women had their zips on the side. Therefore, he deduced, the women also had penises but set on the side of their bodies.

All the girls of the school were in the auditorium that morning and listened without tittering too much as the principal gave a confusing speech about the necessity of knowledge, its negative and positive aspects and how the world had pitfalls. Then followed the film which opened with a man in a suit talking about the necessity of knowledge both positive and negative and the world having pitfalls.

Then various forms of the disease were described using coloured drawings and finally the victims were shown, blank-eyed men and women and even a girl who was blind. Had she gone to prostitutes, I wondered, but before I could ponder the question, a huge breast covered with sores appeared on the screen. All the girls screamed and covered their eyes. This was followed by a screen-sized penis covered with monstrous red sores and we all screamed again in unison. Like most of the audience, I shut my eyes for the remaining thirty minutes and I also stopped up my ears. The screaming continued. Once, when I peeked, naked female genitals were pictured and I screamed with the others and covered my eyes again.

"How yucky," whispered Alena Charlotte to me as we filed out. The line came to a halt and I found myself standing near Mr. L'Abbe, the science teacher, who was glowering red-faced at Mrs. Hutchin.

"Is this your idea of education?" He said in an angry whisper. "You voted in favour of this? Still following your late guru, Mrs. Pankhurst? She would have been proud of you today, showing this stuff to young girls."

Mrs. Hutchin was glaring back and, even though I shuffled a little closer, the line moved on and I did not hear what she said.

At noon, I waited at the side door for Alena Charlotte, so we could walk home together, but I remembered, too late, that she had gone off to the dentist and then, oh horrors, Mrs. Hutchin was bearing down on me. She was a tall boney woman with a long face and heavy eyes. She was wearing the same navy suit and lacc up oxfords she wore every day. A navy hat sat on her grey crimped hair.

THE ART OF BURGLARY

"What luck to catch you, Janet. We can walk along together. I wonder if I could get your opinion of the film. I would be very interested to hear it."

This was worse than I could possibly imagine. I had not intended to talk about the film ever, even with Alena Charlotte, and certainly not with an adult. My plan for the film was to forget about it as quickly as possible. So now, here I was, thinking hard to come up with a response.

"It was very...ah...very...ah...nauseous, "I said at last. Mrs. Hutchin made a sound and I knew she was going to question me further.

"I think that's my mother," I said, indicating some strange women across the street. "So sorry. Good-bye," My black ballerina shoes pounded the sidewalk far ahead of her until I swung through my back door.

Every day that week Alena Charlotte and I snuck home by the back lane to avoid Mrs. Hutchins. We never mentioned the film, nor did any of our girl friends, although Alena Charlotte said her brother and Jack talked of nothing else. To me, it was as if the movie had never happened and I was glad. On Friday afternoon, I walked her home and there, on her porch, was Jack.

"Some movie huh?" he said. Alena Charlotte dived through her front door like a fish into water, but I just glared at him. "Did you like it, huh?" he said.

He was a big black-haired boy with a handsome face and, although lots of girls liked him, I knew he was a bully. He even punched Artie sometimes.

45

Now, he put up his palm, cup shaped, toward my breast. "Woo, woo," he said, moving it back and forth.

"Oh, go play with yourself," I snapped and then a horrible thought hit me. I had heard this expression only once as the tag end of a funny story my cousin Midge was telling her friend. At the time, I thought it was a cute way to tell someone to buzz off, like "oh go jump in the lake." But now I knew what it meant. Sex was in there and I had never noticed it before. Shame hit me like a flood; I, Janet Marsden, had used a bad expression. The effect on Jack was electric.

He backed up across the porch, staring with round dark eyes. "Wow," he said.

I fled.

Two days later, he was at my front door. "Janet," he mumbled so low I had to lean closer, "Would you go to the sock hop with me on Friday?"

My mouth dropped open. I turned and ran upstairs, passing my mother coming down. "Don't want to," I called out to her.

A minute later, from the top of the stairs, I heard her say, "She doesn't want to go out with you, Jack." The front door clicked shut.

I dived under the bed. It was a surprisingly friendly place and I wondered why I had never been there before. The carpet was comfortable, and I reached up for the pillow and pulled it in. Too bad there wasn't enough light for reading.

"I'll come out sometime," I thought, "but not now."

WINE

I skip through the police station door, across the lobby into the back room where the policemen eat their lunches, drop the black metal lunch box on the wooden table, wave to old Sergeant McKee behind the front desk and almost bump into my father in his police uniform when I'm back out on the sidewalk.

"Steady on, lass," he says, leaning down towards me. "Just the gal I want to see. I've something to say to ye, so mark ye well."

My father always looks a bit scary in his uniform. Maybe it's the shadow of the peaked cap that hides his cheery blue eyes. Maybe it's the dark jacket with the golden buttons that make him seem impossibly huge. He puts his hand on my shoulder.

"Ye know that Elsie you play with?" he says. "At the Castle Confectionary on Winder Street."

"What about her?"

"You're to stay away from that store."

"No-o-o." It comes out as a wail.

My father shakes his index finger at me. "Janet, don't blether," he says. "I'm telling ye for your own good—stay away from that store. The place is an outfit and that's all ye need to know."

47

Parents are such difficult people. I nod quickly, "OK, OK." I'm boiling mad. When I get to the corner, I turn and yell, "You're so mean," but he's gone and the double doors of the Port Arthur Police Station are swinging shut.

I kick snow clods as I walk home. I know very well why I have to stay away from the store. Even though Elsie's father is famous in Poland and worked for a newspaper there and was a partisan in the war, here in Canada, he's a bootlegger.

Elsie Dolinski and I became friends three weeks ago when she arrived in our grade four class. She's a fairy girl with sky blue eyes and spun gold hair that wisps across her face. Last week, when it first snowed, she came to school in a white coat with fur trim, white leggings, and carrying a white fur muff. She looked as if she'd stepped off the shelf of the Eaton's doll department.

The first time I go to Elsie's place, we play cut-outs in the big kitchen behind the store. We set our Princess Elizabeth paper dolls on the stairs leading to the bedrooms above. Her mother, a tiny woman with yellowish grey hair in a roll around her head, bustles back and forth from the store to tend to something on the stove. She was a writer in Poland, Elsie tells me, and wrote children's books, but now she's a storekeeper with a big blue apron over her flowered dress. For some reason, she calls me Liddle.

"Here you, Liddle," she says, setting a cup on the table. "Nice you visit my Elsie. Sit, sit and drink this."

THE ART OF BURGLARY

I lift the milky brown liquid to my lips breathing in a magical spicy aroma.

"What is it?" I whisper to Elsie

"Coffee."

The first I've tasted. We only have tea at home and I'm seldom allowed a sip. The forbidden drink tastes dark and woody but I swallow it all. I feel I've passed an important test. I'm a grown-up at last. Wait till my sister hears about this. Meanwhile Mrs. Dolinski is ripping the cellophane from a double pack of Sally Ann cakes. She gives one to each of us. Heaven.

On the next visit, Elsie takes me into the basement, reached from a trap door hidden beneath the kitchen rug. Tiny steps curve down into a stone cellar. Even though the windows are half-blocked with snow, the sunlight weaves a few pale patterns on the floor, giving us enough light to see. I look around the deep stone box. It's like the cave of a mountain troll. In the shadows at one end, the furnace stretches out its many arms, and at the other end, a tower of wooden crates rises to the ceiling. Blue and white bottles on a side table wink at us in the snowy light. But the most interesting items are the five roly-poly wooden barrels, almost as high as me, lined up down the centre of the room. The barrels look like five fat dwarfs. The top of each one is covered with a square of black fabric.

I lift a cloth and lean over the circle of darkness. The smell is thick and sweet, like cough medicine. The liquid comes almost to the top, inky bluish black and shimmering slightly as if an invisible

49

hand is stirring from below. A few tiny bubbles bob up and I quickly drop the cover.

"Isn't this against the law?" I say to Elsie, trying not to sound suspicious. I know all about the bootlegging of wine because I often listen in as my father discusses it with his policeman friends.

"It's for the family. It's not illegal if it's for the family." Clearly Elsie also knows her Criminal Code.

"He's making an awful lot for just one family."

"My papa has a magic potion, and when he uses it, everything is legal."

Before I can ask about the magic potion, her father calls us upstairs. He's set the table with plates and cups. Elsie's mother is not home. It's Sunday and she's at mass. The store is closed.

"Liddle, you want coffee?"

"Yes please."

"Sit here. Eat those donuts."

He sits at the table with us and grins. "In the war, Polish people no got coffee," he says. I'm not sure why that could be a hardship, so I say nothing. "Lotta time, no food, never mind coffee," he goes on.

I feel I'm drinking liquid earth, but I force it down. I'm positive it's making me smarter. I'm turning more grown up every day.

"When you hiding," Elsie's father says, "you so scared, coffee no matter. Even food no matter." He smiles at Elsie and she smiles back. He takes out a pouch and begins rolling a cigarette. "No tobacco either," he says.

I study him. He doesn't look like a war hero. He's hefty and short, and when he walks, moves from side to side. He has on the same thick clothes he wears for his job at the shipyard: heavy black wool pants and layers of plaid shirts. His head seems to grow straight from his shoulders and his mouth is wide. When he grins, and he grins often, I glimpse a gold tooth. A golden grin.

At recess, a week after my dad tells me to stay away from the Castle Confectionary, Elsie asks me to visit the next Sunday afternoon. I smile happily at her because I've figured out a way around my father's orders. It's taken a week of hard thinking. His words, don't go into that store, drum through my mind even when I'm in bed. Then one night, just before sleep, a flash of brain power hits me. I realize he said nothing about going into the kitchen. The kitchen, I reason, is part of the house and a house is not a store. So the kitchen is OK. And, what's more, the store is closed on Sundays, so I couldn't go into the store even if I wanted to.

"I'll be over after lunch on Sunday," I say.

We head for the basement, immediately closing the trap behind us. However, just as we reach the bottom of the stairs, we hear the blast of a whistle. Big black boots run through the snow outside the windows and heavy thumps come from overhead. I climb on a wooden crate and look out. Three policemen are lined up across the back yard. Chief Reynolds is waving his arms and blowing a whistle.

Elsie begins to spin in a dithering circle. She's wailing. "Police. No, no. Hide, hide."

She pushes me behind the pile of crates and dives in after me just as a square of light speeds across the floor and the trap is flung open with a crash. We crouch like mice against the stone wall. Elsie has her head down in her hands, but I can see everything through the wooden slats. To my horror, the police chief, followed by my father and Sergeant McKee, runs down the narrow steps.

Mr. Dolinski runs after them, talking fast. "Not vine, No, no. No vine. Never. Ween gart. Ween."

The chief strides to a barrel and tosses off the cloth. He sticks in his finger and tastes. "Right. Here's the evidence and lots of it. There's enough wine here for the Russian army. This should convict our Pollock friend." He turns to my father, "Marsden!"

"Yes, sir."

"Get upstairs on the phone. Tell Banning to send the truck to haul this stuff away." My father clatters up the stairs.

While the chief is throwing the cloth covers on the floor and tasting the contents of each barrel with his finger, old Sergeant McKee is stalking around the basement. He picks up two bottles from the table and puts them in his jacket pockets. He puts two more bottles under one arm. He then heads toward our end of the room. When he gets to the crates, he looks directly at them, and I'm sure he sees us through the slats. I shrink even smaller thinking this is the way a mouse feels when it's cornered by the cat. The chief is now halfway up the stairs and yells, "Come along, McKee!"

THE ART OF BURGLARY

Elsie's father is now alone in the centre of the room. When Elsie crawls out, he shakes his head at her and waves her back in. For such a burly man he moves fast, taking a glass bottle from a shelf and splashing liquid into each barrel.

"It's the magic potion," Elsie whispers to me. A nasty sharp smell slowly pervades the room. I cover my mouth and nose, but the sickening odour moves through my fingers and into my head.

I can hear Mr. Dolinski shouting as he runs back upstairs. "Come down, police. Come down, police. Ween gart, ween gart." When he reappears a minute later with old Sergeant McKee, he's still yelling. "See, ween gart. I make to sell in store."

"What the hell," says Sergeant McKee. "What a stink. It smells like..."

He sticks a finger in the closest barrel and tastes. "Vinegar. God in heaven, it's vinegar." He puts a finger in each barrel. "All vinegar."

"I sell in store," says Elsie's father. "Good ween gart."

"Christ." McKee turns and runs up the stairs.

Next, Chief Reynolds comes down, tastes the first barrel, makes a face and retreats. Mr. Dolinski follows him up the stairs, one hand behind his back flapping at us to stay in hiding. Boots bang and thump above with a lot of yelling mixed in. After a long time, I hear the roar of motors in the back lane and I know they've left at last. We creep out on our hands and knees. Elsie's face is streaked with dust and tears. She flies up the stairs crying for her father. I follow. No one is in the kitchen, but, through the open door to the store, I see Mr.

53

Dolinski looking out the big window, his large arm around Elsie's shoulders. He's grinning.

I grab my coat from the pile in the back shed, and shoot outside like a bird from a trap.

My father can't stop laughing. My sister and I, in the kitchen doing the supper dishes, see him through the open door to the living room. "Why the old man left him alone in the basement, I'll never know," my father says. "Leaving him with the wine. And the crafty fella just splashed some vinegar in each barrel and that turns everything to vinegar. You canna arrest someone for making vinegar."

"Didn't he have some bottles of wine already made up?" says my Uncle Everett. He and my Aunt Sissy are over for Sunday supper.

"Oh, family use. Can't get a conviction on three or four bottles."

Aunt Sissy speaks next. "I don't see why you're bothering poor immigrants at a'. Aren't they just trying to get along? And on a Sunday an a'."

"Och, no, Sissy. We're not such monsters, and on a Sunday the wife and kiddy go off to church, so we spared them the upset. But Chief Reynolds loves a raid." He starts to laugh again, slapping his knee. "When the lads at the Fort William station hear about this…"

Sergeant McKee and a young policeman called Constable Aduno are at the front door. McKee carries two Eaton's shopping bags that he lifts into the air as he steps inside. "Ween gart," he calls out.

My mother comes into the kitchen. "Leave the dishes, girls. Come and try a sip of wine." I toss the dish towel on the rack. There's never been wine in the house as far as I remember. My mother makes us carry out some cups and water glasses on the tea tray. Constable Aduno opens a bottle using a twisty metal tool he takes from his pocket. When Sergeant McKee looks at me, he gives me a big wink. I quickly look at the floor.

"To the Poles," says Sergeant McKee, raising his glass. "God bless them."

Constable Aduno takes a sip. "Not bad. The old con artist knew what he was doing." He takes a gulp. "Excellent. He could've been Italian."

I taste a bitty drop from my teacup. Sour. My sister is making a screwed up face and sticking out her tongue. This stuff tastes worse than the vinegar smelled, worse than coffee, worse than the worst medicine, worse than dandelion juice.

My aunt and mother are also unimpressed.

"I'd rather have a nice cup of tea," says Aunt Sissy.

In bed that night, it sounds as if a grown-up party is going full swing downstairs. Aunt Sissy sings, "Stop your Ticklin', Jock," her special party song. My mother sings, "The Little Red Hen" and my Uncle Everett belts out, "The Biggest Aspidistra in the World," my favourite of all the grown-up songs. I can hear my father laughing. Every once in a while I catch old Sergeant McKee's voice chanting, "Ween gart, ween gart." If he spied me

55

behind the crates, he didn't tell my father. I send him a million thought messages. Thank you, thank you.

I think about Elsie. Did I ever mention to her my dad was a policeman? I don't recall, but she's sure to find out one day. Until then, there's a chance for more coffee and treats at the Castle Confectionary.

I snuggle into the blankets. My sister snores beside me with her mouth open. Sleep slides over me like a magic spell.

GRACE STREET

The streets of Port Arthur go uphill and down and behind them, hidden, are the back lanes, even more twisted than the streets. Often, they run through fields or around rocky outcroppings. Sometimes there are houses back there, shacks, or garages that were turned into houses during the war and sometimes regular houses all alone on a long stretch of lane like boats cast up by the waves.

Glady's house is like this. It's perched on a stretch of flat rock behind Grace Street. I am passing it now on my way to the police station to deliver my father's lunch. It's an unpainted two-storey that leans slightly. Glady and her family, her mother and two older brothers, moved in about a month ago.

Last Thursday, after school, my friend Elsie and I went with Glady to play in her house. It's an interesting place. For instance, there is hardly any furniture. Glady has a big room to herself, the lucky duck, and she sleeps in her own bed. She keeps her clothes in cardboard boxes lined up along the wall, a neat way to do it, I think.

We three girls run around screaming, in and out the empty rooms. When we get to the bedrooms of Glady's brothers, we jump up and down on their mattresses, which are on the floor. We land on our knees and then with another leap, land on our backs, rumpling the smoothed blankets. The elder brother, Albert, has movie star pictures tacked to the wall, so we take a crayon and draw mustaches on Rita Hayworth and Carmen Miranda. Henry, the second brother, has a pile of Batman comics beside his bed, and these we fan out and hide under his mattress.

One of the cardboard boxes in Henry's room contains a pair of pants and a blue plaid shirt, white with dust. "My brothers work at the elevators shovelling grain," Glady says. "Watch." She picks up the shirt, tosses it into the air, and grain dust like tiny snowflakes fills the sunlight, and makes haloes around our heads. We throw up our arms and dance in the pretend snow as Glady flaps the shirt up and down. A thin sheen settles on the dark linoleum and I write DUSTY in it with my finger and then, boldly, LOVE, JANET, and this gives us the giggles.

We pelt down the back stairs and up the front stairs, stopping at the landing halfway to peek through a place in the wall that has a hole to the outside, a spy hole, where we can check on the world, although there's nothing to see—just the wide flat rocks and patches of grass that take up the area behind Grace Street. On the third circuit, we spy Glady's mother huffing up the lane from the hospital where she has just finished her shift in the kitchens.

Life is so strange, I think now, as I study the house on the way to the police station. For

THE ART OF BURGLARY

example, how come I didn't know, until just a few hours ago, that Glady is Indigenous?

I learn this fact in our kitchen that very morning. My sister and I are waiting for the scones to come out of the oven and my Aunt Sissy, who has dropped in for tea, is there too. I stand snuggled up beside her and show her my Grade Four class list that we copied from the board so we get to know each other for the new school year. My Aunt Sissy is squashy and warm and has a droopy face that smiles a lot. It's odd that she's so different from my mother, who's as tall and bony as a skeleton. I'm sure if my mother ever hugged me, I'd feel squashed by sticks.

My mother turns from the counter where she's packing up the lunch pail and, using her long apron, opens the high oven door to lift out the sheet of scones, carefully sliding them onto the big Blue Willow platter in the middle of the table. My sister grabs one and juggles it in her hands, waiting for it to cool.

"How do you say that name, Janet?" My Aunt Sissy points to Elsie's last name.

"Na-tish-in," I say.

My aunt sighs, running her eyes down the list. "Tolvanen, Ho, LaBrie, Andropoulus," she reads aloud. "Do none of them have proper names, then, Meg?" she says to my mother.

"Not in our Janet's class," says my mother. She's wrapping a piece of cold pork pie in a waxed bread wrapper and placing it into the black metal box. "Nary an English name in the school, much less a Scot's." She polishes an apple on her apron and places it inside. "She's even got a girl from the Reserve in her class."

"I do?" I almost drop the table knife I'm using to slather butter on a scone.

"That Glady you play with," my mother says.

My aunt searches down the list. "Gladys Sky," she reads and frowns. "How can that be, Meg, for mark ye this. I know for a fact that no Indigenous person is allowed past Marshall-Wells." Marshall-Wells is the big hardware store on the edge of the downtown. "They're to stay down the South End and not come up town at a'. That's why their kids go to King George's, down the coal docks. Them that go, of course."

"Glady's family lives up here now," I say, "in the lane behind Grace Street." I want to describe the swell house, but I decide it's more important to cram in a second scone.

"Huh." My mother looks at my aunt while giving her little grunt of disapproval. "An unwritten law. Supposedly it's been that way for a long time." She snaps the thermos inside the domed lid and closes the box by clicking the metal snaps. My dad's initials, D.M. for Duncan Marston, shine out in yellow paint from the side and she gives them a rub with her apron.

"So," my aunt says softly, "a chance taken. Good for them. I don't abide them sort of rules, as ye know. We dinna come to Canada, Meg, to live by unwritten laws."

I want to hear more, but my mother gives me a little push towards the door "Dinna dawdle," she says and I take off, over to Grace Street and down

THE ART OF BURGLARY

❖

I do dawdle, for now I'm studying Glady's house, trying to think what she looks like. She's taller than me and stronger too, with a square face and a big smile. Her hair is darker than mine but just as straight and cut short with bangs across the front, while my hair is always plaited into two annoying pigtails that hang down my back. My mind turns to Elsie, who I know is Polish, and I recall her thin pointed face, very pretty, baby blue eyes, and mousy hair falling over her face so that she's always blowing the strands away.

Each person in the world looks different, I think, and yet, at the same time, they look like the place they came from. On the other hand, Glady doesn't look at all like those big brothers of hers. My mind turns to Aunt Sissy and my mother, sisters and Scottish but very different looking.

My thoughts are interrupted by a slamming noise and Glady's mother stumps down the front steps. She seems to be looking for something, for her head swivels from side to side as she scans the flat rocks in front of the house and the lane in both directions.

I give her a big wave. "Hi, Mrs. Sky." She narrows her eyes at me until they are two dark slits with black eyebrows shoved down over them. A big U-shaped frown takes up the bottom half of her face. Suddenly she looks as scary as a Hallowe'en witch

61

and I step back in alarm, while trying another wave. "Hi, Hi," I say, sort of stuttering. Her hand shoots out towards me in a 'go away' gesture, and she turns abruptly to stand looking in the other direction.

What did I do? I'm stunned. Then Rita Hayworth's mustache flashes into my mind. *Good gravy! Trouble!* When in danger, I remind myself, *run away.* And I do, fleeing down the lane in a panic yelling "ah, ah, ah" until I reach the shortcut through the hospital grounds, where I stop yelling in case the nuns hear me and come out to chase me off the property.

I've brought Dad's lunch to the police station many times. It's a scary place, but I'm used to it. The double front doors are made of golden oak and could've been beautiful except they're stained with black streaks along the grain. They're usually propped half-open winter and summer and are so now. The three stone steps up to them dip down in the middle "carved out by people's reluctant feet," my father once said. I stop on the top step and carefully check all around the oak door frame inside and out and across the speckled marble floor inside. I'm looking for cockroaches. The place is infested with them and my father and his policemen friends often make jokes about them. I've never seen one and I don't want to see one either. I study the speckles, watching for any movement and, when I see none, skip forward.

The room isn't large. Directly across from the door is a long black bench, like a bench in church, and quite often there are men sitting there. There are two men there now, in the usual posture, bent forward, legs wide apart, arms on knees and faces looking at the floor. On the right side is a wooden counter higher than my head with a metal grill along the top. There's always a policeman behind there, I know. On the left, a wide black staircase winds up into the shadows. It leads to the courtroom on the second floor and once, when there was no court going on, my father took my sister and me up to have a look. It was a big room, with a strange sweaty smell, and as hushed as a church. We stared at the king's picture and the Union Jack and the rows of empty benches with the judge's desk high above all, like the throne of a fairy-tale king.

The door to the policemen's lunchroom is on the first floor behind the staircase and it's there, on a long table down the middle, I deposit the lunch box.

My father stands at the end of the room talking to his friend, old Sergeant McKee, who, to me, looks way too old to be a policeman. At first they don't see me. "It's not right, for all that, Donald," I hear my father say and the sergeant answers, "Leave it, Duncan lad. You'll not change his mind and ye know it. We've got other tasks ahead of us, to get organized," and I know from his hushed voice he's referring to the union my dad is trying to get started among the policemen. "Oncet we get a bit of protection, then, and only then, can we make some changes."

The union is a dark secret, the deepest secret of all, and must never be mentioned to anyone, not even to Aunt Sissy. I only learned of it by listening at the top of the stairs after I was supposed to be in bed. It's a shame my father's ears are so sharp for he heard me trying to sneak back up. He yelled, which he hardly ever does, and warned me a lot. Terrible punishments would happen if I blabbed. I'd have to stay in the house for a week, for example, and not have any dessert. If the Police Chief found out, my dad could be fired and then we'd all starve or, even worse, have to go back to Scotland.

So, now I pretend not to hear their conversation and just say, "Hi, Pops."

My father is a big guy who looks like a boxer. He's got sandy hair and sandy freckled skin that reaches way past his forehead. Every week or so, I notice his forehead getting higher because he gets a little balder every day. His nose and ears are too big. His eyes are as blue as Lake Superior on a sunny day. His mustache is so blond and thin, it's hard to see unless you stand close up. Since he became a detective and started working 'plain clothes,' he wears the same brown suit every day.

"Here you are, Janet," he says leaning down to put his hand on my upper arm. "Right now, it might be best if I walk you out," he says and leads me to the lunchroom door.

A loud voice outside the room stops us. "Get the hell out," it says. "I'm letting you off this time. I think you get the picture well enough." The voice has changed into a scary sneering tone. Leaning around my dad's legs, I can see Chief Reynolds, my father's enemy in the fight for the union. Immediately, my dad draws me back into the lunch room. I can see the chief looming over the two men on the bench, and when they lift their heads, I'm amazed to see Henry and Albert, Glady's brothers. Their faces are as closed as the rock in front of their house, but I can tell by their hunched-up shoulders they're angry. "I've explained it so even you dummies should be able to understand," the chief goes on. "If we pick you up again, it'll be the cells for a night or two." His voice grows even louder. "That's a promise, do you hear, dick-heads? So, if you want to keep those jobs, stay in your own part of town."

The two young men stand up together, towering over the chief and, for an instant, I'm afraid there'll be a fight, but I notice that the desk sergeant has come around and is standing beside his boss, in his hand the leaded blackjack that all the cops carry. Albert moves first, walking quickly toward the front door. After balancing on his toes for a minute, Henry follows.

My father waits until the chief goes back behind the counter to his office and waits longer until he hears the office door slam.

My heart is thumping and I feel hot, as if I've been standing in the sun. "That's Albert and Henry, my girlfriend's brothers," I cry. "What did they do?"

My father is sharp. "No business of yours," he says as he walks me out to the sidewalk. "Now, Janet," he says curving his big finger at me, "you remember that you're not to say a word of police business to anyone. Not anyone. Never. Not to your friend either. Do ye understand me?"

I nod. My stomach squeezes into a big twist and my heart jumps up and down like a frightened rabbit.

"Good girl," he says." Off with you now. And Janet..." I turn. "Thanks for bringing the lunch."

I figure it out on the way home. It's obvious. Albert and Henry broke the unwritten law. They were caught in the wrong part of town. What will they do now? How can they go to work if they live up the hill and not down in the South End? How can they live in their house? Life is so mean, I think, and dumb too. The unwritten law isn't fair, but, as hard as I try, I can't think what to do about it.

When I complain to my father he merely says, "Aye, it's wrong and it'll be changed one day. Not now, Lass. Not yet."

On Monday, at recess, Glady pulls me behind the caragana hedge at the edge of the playground. "My mother says she's sorry for scaring you," she whispers so no one else can hear. "She was worried because the boys were late, is all." Then she laughs. "She says you'll grow wings one day, you're so speedy."

I blurt out, "How are your brothers?"

"They've left," Glady says, "because of what happened at the police station. You know what I mean," she says and then laughs again. "Henry's got a bad temper so Ma thinks he'll get in trouble if he stays here."

I'm shocked, unable to speak. The boys must've recognized me at the police station and then mentioned it to their mother and Glady. At the

THE ART OF BURGLARY

time, I didn't think their eyes had come my way once.

"They're going back north to trap for the winter," Glady says, "so the house is way too big for us now. We're moving in with my Grandma in Fort William."

"Fort William! So far away!" Before she can answer, the bell shrills out and we have to run to get in line. I turn to see Glady, but she isn't there. My eyes search the lines, looking for black hair and bangs and a big happy face, but she has vanished the way angels do in the Bible. Silently and completely.

After school, I recruit Elsie and my sister to come with me to Glady's house, because I'm still afraid of her mother and I need reinforcements. I want to say good-bye. But when we turn down the lane, we hear the front door banging in the wind. The place has a hollow look and the windows are skull eyes. Our knocking sends clunky sounds into the emptiness inside.

We creep in, holding hands, our feet scuffling along as we try to be quiet in case someone is here. Close together and moving across the wooden floors in the bare downstairs rooms, which never did have any furniture, we go into the kitchen to find only the wood stove and the stained yellow linoleum remain. The cupboard doors hang open to reveal bare shelves. Even the dish pan is gone and the bag of clothes-pins by the back door.

Upstairs in Glady's room, the cardboard boxes, still carefully lined up along the walls, gape empty. Glady's bed is missing, but the boys' mattresses still lie on the floor. Before, the house always smelled

67

faintly of bleach, but now a damp odour is creeping through the rooms. Rita Hayworth, looking over one bare shoulder and showing her mustache, is still on Albert's wall. I rip her down, crumple her up and throw her in the corner and then do the same with Carmen Miranda and her stupid smile and headdress of fruit. In the next room, I roll back Henry's mattress and there are the Batman comics. We kneel on the linoleum, still powdered with grain dust, and divide them among us. Then, without talking about it, we clutch the comics and run outside as fast as we can.

That night, my father doesn't come home for supper and my mother paces the kitchen, wiping down the counter over and over, washing each dish as soon as my sister and I finish with it. When she orders us to bed at seven o'clock, much too early, we go without complaint because first, you can't argue with my mother and second, we've got the Batman comics. We sit up in bed and go through them all, passing them over as soon as we have one finished. Eventually, my sister falls asleep, but I can still hear my mother pacing between the kitchen and the living room.

"The English bastard!" My mother's voice wakes me. It's still light outside so I couldn't have slept long. I never heard her use a bad word before so I've got to hear more. I creep to the top of the stairs.

"A year! A year on the night shift. And back to the beat just when ye've moved into plain clothes. The bastard."

THE ART OF BURGLARY

"Ah, aye," my father sighs. "But mind, he doesn't know for sure; he just suspects. Good may come from it, however. Maybe this incident will get the waverers thinking so they sign that paper. I've no doubt, Meg, we'll be certified before the year is up and then I'll be all right but till then..."

His voice trails off and there's a long silence. "Our Janet will be happy anyway," he says with a laugh. "I'll be down in the South End and maybe we can do something about that so-called unwritten law."

"Oh, do be careful, Duncan," my mother says.

There's another silence and then he says, so softly that I have to move down a couple of steps to hear it, "Are ye afraid, Meg? Ye know that Reynolds will be snooping round and if he gets any real facts about the union, he'll fire me. He said as much today. So are ye afraid? Do you want me to stop? Say the word."

"Afraid?" my mother says. "Stop? Bow to that black-hearted Englishman? Huh! We can wait him out, Duncan. Aye and best him in the end. Come on, my dear, and get your tea. Come on Duncan now, and get your tea."

THE ART OF BURGLARY

"The arch," said Rose Garton, "is a powerful shape. That's what my father says. That's why he's taking off all the doors in the house and building arches instead."

Taking off all the doors? My sister and I moved closer. "Why is the arch so powerful?" I asked.

"I don't know, Janet, but now we have a big arch over the kitchen sink."

It was June 1950. Rose and Hyacinth Garton, newcomers to our Port Arthur neighbourhood, were the same age as my sister, Leanna and I, eight and ten years old and just as ragged. Their mother, when I saw her outside, looked pale and tired. I attributed this to the weirdness of the father's personality.

He did not have a job but spent his days remodelling their old house, which sat directly across the street from ours. By the middle of June, we heard he'd painted all the kitchen cupboards in rainbow colours. A neighbourhood rumour claimed he'd taken off the bathroom door and replaced it with an arch. I was dying to find out if this were true.

"Can I go in your house to use the bathroom?" I asked Hyacinth with my fingers crossed behind my

THE ART OF BURGLARY

back to cancel out the fib. "Our house is locked and my mother won't open the door."

She was not at all suspicious but let me in, calling out to her mother in the kitchen. "Janet's going to the bathroom, OK?"

I nipped up the stairs and, moving quickly along the hallway, I noted the three bedroom doors were missing, replaced by plastered and painted arches, a yellow one, a deep blue and a bright green—gashes of colour against the grey wallpaper of the upstairs hall. A quick peek in each room showed me the closet doors were also missing. A large rainbow arch stretched over the bed in the biggest bedroom. Thankfully, the bathroom door was still intact.

I moved downstairs as quietly as I could. The entrance to the living room was crowned by a sweeping arch of chunky white plaster. The desire to explore gripped me. I looked around. Hyacinth had vanished, but I could hear dishwashing noises coming from the kitchen at the back of the house. I rocked in indecision, twisting the cotton skirt of my play dress into a ball and then made up my mind. If anyone asked, I would say I was looking for my friend.

I stepped into the living room. The high front window sent dusty sunlight over the white sheets covering the furniture. Newspapers were scattered across the hardwood floor. They slithered softly as I tiptoed forward. A smell like old paste filled the room.

The fireplace was surrounded by green glass tiles set into the wall, but the mantel above was missing, replaced by a rounded gash showing a wire grid with pieces of plaster and wallpaper sticking to it. The mantel itself was sprawled across the white-sheeted chesterfield. It was made of golden oak, my favourite wood. Alas, it had been sawn into three lengths. I supposed an arch would eventually replace it.

I felt sad about the mantel, but, on the other hand, I could sense a master plan behind the destruction. Some force was stirring up Mr. Garton's brain. I imagined a giant swirl inside it spinning coloured visions and streaming them out so fast they shot from his hands like forked lightning, sending him racking and ruining around the house trying to force everything into a pattern. The man was strange, no doubt about it—even for our neighbourhood. But he was full of ideas.

Later, when I told my parents about the arches and the mantel, they were extremely interested and questioned me at length. "A perfectly good house ruined for naught," my mother said. "What a dog's breakfast!"

My father clapped a hand to his forehead. "Another haywire artist," he said.

But I didn't tell them everything. I didn't tell them that I'd tiptoed about for a long time and even ventured into the dining room. I didn't tell them about the painting on the dining room wall. This information I saved for my sister and my friend, Alana Charlotte.

"Talk about beautiful," I told them. "Real huge. It takes up the whole wall. "In the middle," I paused, "is this beautiful lady wearing a long Greek goddess

THE ART OF BURGLARY

dress." I made a trailing motion with my hands. "A twisty gold headband too." I traced a circle around my own forehead. "She's standing on a white balcony beside a big flower pot with lilies in it and —get this—a peacock stands beside her with its green tail sweeping across the floor. She's got one hand resting on the peacock's head and one hand on a marble pillar, while she looks out to blue mountains far away."

My audience, standing around me in a circle, was listening carefully, their eyes round. I dropped my voice to a whisper. "It's the most beautiful picture I've ever seen."

"Holy Dinah!" Alana Charlotte said. "How could such beauty have found its way to our neighbourhood?"

The question now was how to get inside to take another look, but the Garton girls took in no visitors no matter how much we hinted.

"My dad's a genius," Rose Garton told me one day as I was kneeling on the sidewalk, carefully drawing a hopscotch using different coloured chalk.

"Hokey Doodle," I said. "Who says?"

"He is too. He paints big pictures. He's got lots in the back shed, ready to move into the house when the arches are finished. So, put that in your pipe and smoke it!" I did not answer and, a minute later, she ran off.

Good gravy, I thought, sitting back on my heels. A treasure hoard of paintings in a back shed. But how to break in to see them?

It turned out to be easy. The entire Garton family had left for the day on a mysterious errand— 'to collect coloured bottles,' according to Rose. Examining the shed closely, my sister and I noted a space between it and the old fence behind it. It was a snap to slip in there. The single half-broken window was so dusty we couldn't see inside. We carefully removed the big pieces of glass, set them on the ground, and climbed in.

A big painting was hanging on the wall, a half finished version of the peacock lady I'd seen inside the house. Several long rolls of canvas were piled on the floor. They were too large for us to unroll in such a small space where every inch was jammed with old paint cans.

In bed, I pondered those rolled-up pictures. What lovely scenes did they hide? But I reminded myself, removing one from the shed would be stealing. Besides, someone was sure to see. And even if we got one roll outside, where could we hook up an edge to open it? I turned over idea after idea, without success. However, a few days later, something happened that made me forget this puzzle. A new opportunity presented itself that tossed the paintings right out of my brain.

My Aunt Sissy was visiting and, as usual, she and my mother were reading the tea leaves.

"Do ye see an interior decorator for me in there at a'?" My Auntie Sissy laughed, staring into her cup. "I could use one around my place."

My mother carefully dripped out the excess liquid into the saucer and slowly turned the cup around three times. "Eh, you're daft, you are," she said, but she was laughing as she peered at the leaves. "I can see a fancy iron gate at the door of your living room," she joked. "And our Janet swinging on it like a monkey."

My ears tuned in when I heard my name. I put Nancy Drew aside. "Who's got an iron gate?" I said.

"The Moore's up the street," said my mother. "They hired an interior decorator. They say he's made all the rooms the same colour. "My," she sighed, "some folk ha' money to burn."

Something in my heart glowed at the mention of the iron gate and the rooms all the same colour. I knew the Moore's had gone off to summer camp as had the Gordon's, their nearest neighbour. It would be easy to slip inside the newly decorated house.

Early the next morning, I crouched in the tangle of bushes against the stone basement wall, studying a small window. The outer storm section was easily removed by twisting the wing-like edges of the four screws, which held it in place. I carefully put it behind the bushes. The interior pane swung in from hinges at the top. Below was some sort of table or workbench and I dropped inside.

Like most basements, the space was taken up by the coal furnace, a monster of many pipes like a giant octopus. The coal cellar was just beyond and, piles of kindling, the preserve cupboard, and general junk took up the rest of the area.

On the main floor, the kitchen was even more old fashioned than ours, but, moving into the front hall, I stopped, astounded. A lovely house awaited me. The large entry room was tiled in black and white like a mansion in a movie. At the far end hung the celebrated gate made of a decorative metal as curly as a fancy bookplate. It swung open noiselessly as I stepped into the living room. Colours enveloped me. I took in the furniture, walls, and rugs. Everything was pale green and cream, even the vases on the mantel and the picture over it of a lady in a long slinky dress.

Upstairs, I checked out the two boys' bedrooms —uninteresting—but the master bedroom was different. It shimmered in pale peach and cream. The counterpane, walls, curtains, rugs and the skirt of Mrs. Moore's dressing table all matched. I did not go into the room but just stood in the doorway and enjoyed it. I felt I was drinking colour.

The master bedroom sat at one end of the long upstairs hall. At the opposite end was a door, which opened to a set of stairs leading to the attic, a single large room fitted out as the bedroom for the teen-age twins. It was as uninteresting as the boys' rooms on the second floor.

I do not think I was inside the house more than ten minutes. Moving quickly, I headed for the basement and once outside, replaced the storm window, closed the screws, checked about and left. My housebreaking feat had been successfully accomplished.

During the month of July, I broke into several houses alone, always going through a basement window, but none was as interesting or beautiful as the Moore's place. During these housebreaking forays, I touched nothing—except the odd door knob—and stole nothing. I was not there to steal but rather to satisfy my curiosity about the inside.

THE ART OF BURGLARY

I did not break into the houses of my friends but into the "odd houses," those owned by older people without children or whose children had grown up. I was taking great chances, for I did not know these people well and could only guess they'd gone off to summer camp or were out for the day. Luckily, I was never caught, but a group of us came very close on the next foray into the Moore's.

There were four of us, my sister and I plus my friend Alana Charlotte and her twin brother Artie. We'd just reached the third floor, the attic bedroom of the teen-aged twins, when we heard a car pull up and its doors slam. To our stricken ears, the kitchen door opened and the voices of Mr. and Mrs. Moore floated up from the first floor far below. We were statues, unable to whisper to each other and unable to move. Footsteps came up the main staircase along with talk and laughter. It seemed to us the steps went into the main bedroom. We stood staring at each other. Finally, I beckoned the gang forward, carefully tiptoeing down with the others behind me. Very slowly, I pushed open the narrow door to the upstairs hall.

All was quiet except for a curious creaking noise. As we stole along toward the main staircase, we could see down the hall into the main bedroom to the bed where a naked rear end was moving up and down. It was just a glimpse, but I had an impression of dark hair on a large, hairy rump.

We moved on, barely breathing, down the steps, across the black-and-white tiled entry to the kitchen, down to the basement and, one at a time, climbed up on the worktable, out the window and into the bushes. As the last person out, I replaced the window as usual.

We never talked to each other about the curious scene in the bedroom and I never knew if the others had seen it as well. To me, it looked like some sort of physical exercise. But our close call scared me. I never broke into a house again.

Mr. Garton, perhaps tired of building arches inside his house, had moved his decorating project outside. He began by collecting glass bottles and sorting them into different-coloured piles. There were blue Pepto-Bismol bottles, green Pepsi bottles, and other piles of yellow, orange, and red. He broke them up with a hammer so that he had several large mounds of glass pieces organized in his side yard.

His plan was to cover his house in coloured glass shapes. Each morning he set up a tall ladder. Next, he made a fire in the yard and heated up a pail of tar. After much upping and downing on the ladder, he cut out and fitted a jig-saw shaped piece of beaver board, in size about three feet long. Once he had the shape correct, he smeared it with tar and sprinkled the glass of a single colour onto it. After letting it dry a few minutes, he climbed up and nailed it in place.

The work was so time consuming, especially the shaping of the pieces, that by the end of September he had only covered part of the front wall. We kids often stood on the sidewalk and watched him as he laboured on, but my father, looking across the street from behind the net curtains of our front windows, was not a fan. "What the hell?" he said. "The man's insane."

My mother had many chats with the neighbours. "Too bad we can't get the city to do something," she said. "It's a right enough disgrace." Many nods in agreement.

But I admired Mr. Garton, even though I was sorry for him too. It was clear to me that he had a vision to create a sparkly glass house. Unfortunately, I realized artistic vision is often not enough, for, in spite of the grinding work, that idea ended up a complete flop because what one saw, from a distance, was a house covered with tar and even close up, the bits of glass reflected more black than colour.

THE LOVER

Sometimes it takes years before you understand the meaning of a glance. And further years may pass before you understand anything at all about the tangled landscape of love.

At the time of the glance, I am fourteen years old. On a bright June day, I run up the street, through the gap in the lilac hedge. It's seven in the morning and I am two hours early, but I focus only on the doctor who, on Saturday mornings, usually spends an hour or two in his iris garden before he drives down to the family's summer cottage on Lake Superior. His wife and elder daughter, Holly, have been living there for the past two weeks, ever since Holly finished grade twelve. I am sparking with happiness because Mimi, the doctor's younger daughter and my best friend, has invited me to the cottage for the weekend.

My Eaton's shopping bag containing pyjamas, sweater, and my old bathing suit swings against the branches as I skimble through the hedge. And there's the doctor, kneeling among the irises. My breath flies out in a big huff of happiness.

He sees me at once. "Here's the early riser," he says as hc always does. "Come on Janet. Look at the newest beauty."

The irises dot the wide curving bed which takes up most of the front yard. The few that are in flower are all deep blue or purple. Some have silver veins fanning from their down-turned lips. But the doctor points to a fat yellow bud still partly enclosed in its green coat.

"It's golden," I say. "How wonderful."

He strokes the folded petals. "It'll swell out tonight."

"What's its name?" I kneel down beside him.

"Haven't found out yet. I'm thinking of calling it, temporarily, Dorion Gold," he says, picking up the garden claw and scrabbling at the nearby weeds. "Spied it last year at an abandoned farm in Dorion. I could see the petals blazing from the road. It was buried up to its neck in quack grass but still blooming like the sun. Obviously a vigorous old bird, eh? Sort of like me actually, when you come to think about it."

He smiles at me with his sparkly smile. "So what do you think, Janet? Dorion Gold? A good enough name?"

I take a chance. "If it's like you," I say slowly, "why not call it the Doctor Gordon Iris? Or even better, the Garnet Gold." I love the doctor's melodious first name and, in my daydreams, always call him Garnet.

Doctor Garnet Gordon is a big-shouldered guy with silver hair and a square handsome face. He has very white teeth and, when I'm close to him, I can smell his antiseptic doctor soap. Sometimes, in my daydreams, he's my husband; we dine together in his walnut-panelled dining room, chatting merrily and the maid, whose name is Scotty, is serving us. Sometimes, he's my father; we are out for a ride in the car and he stops to buy me a chocolate ice cream cone. Sometimes, he's my best friend and we are walking along a bush path together as if we have all the time in the world. He tells me about being a doctor in the army. He tells me about heritage roses and the difference between bearded and Siberian irises. And I talk a lot too, about school and the books I am reading and—this is the best part—he listens carefully and asks me questions in his easy pleasant voice. These dreams spin around me in a hundred different guises; they are the cocoon in which I live.

But he's not listening now. He has leapt to his feet at the sight of a tall girl striding across the lawn. She's wearing white tennis clothes and swinging a racket in one hand while holding, in the other, a large pink valise. She has a fuzzy pink band across her blond pageboy and a pink sweater over her shoulders. I know who she is. Her name is Regina Vale and she's Holly's friend and tennis partner, both entered in the tournament this weekend at the cottage.

The doctor turns to me and puts the garden claw into my hand. "Why don't you toss this thing into the basket on the porch, Janet? Then go off and find that Mimi. Throw her out of bed if you have to. Tell her that her fond papa says to get a move on. And tell Scotty we'll leave in thirty minutes."

THE ART OF BURGLARY

He smiles at Regina, who is waving her racket at him. "So, Regina, you're all ready for the courts," he says.

"I want to start practicing as soon as we get there," I hear her say. "Oh, gee, we do need it. We're awfully bad, Doctor Gordon. We're bound to be eliminated right off. It's going to be so darn embarrassing." She gives a squeaky giggle.

As I head up the front steps, I hear his easy laugh and see him take her valise in one hand and, with the other, replace the top corner of her sweater that has slipped from her shoulder.

Later in the car, squeezed in the front seat between Regina and the door, I learn that Mimi is to be in the tournament as well. My friend sits alone in the back seat among the bags, tennis rackets, and suitcases. The trunk of the car is taken up with five rose bushes wrapped in burlap and two cases of beer. She complains bitterly.

"I don't know why you signed me up. I'm not very good and Janet can't even play tennis; she doesn't even have a racket so what will she do—just stand there?"

The doctor laughs. "Oh, she can be our cheer leader. And she can help me plant these roses. And maybe you can lend a hand, Regina?" And he pats her on the knee just before he shifts the gears to slow down at the House of Ice so we can all get chocolate ice cream cones.

At the cottage, Mimi and I bolt from the car as soon as it stops. First, Mimi flies into the arms of her mother, a neat grey-haired woman in wire-rimmed glasses and a flowered dress who is waiting in the drive. "Love you, Mummsy," she says, nuzzling into her. "Missed you scads." Mimi's big sister Holly, a taller version of her mother with the same wire-rimmed specs and crimped hair is there too, ignoring us but greeting Regina with happy cries. Mimi and I dance off to change into our bathing suits in Holly's bedroom.

The Gordon cottage consists of one big room with a set of small bedrooms lined up along one side. A screen porch extends across the front and a narrow kitchen stretches along the back. Although we change in Holly's room for privacy, we won't sleep there. We sleep in the mezzanine, an interior balcony overlooking the main room and reached by a ladder. I have slept up there before and now, as we climb up to stow our gear, I can see the blue lake beyond the screens and smell its sweet vanilla smell.

As always, the water in Lake Superior is brutally cold, but, when I surface, I feel encased in colour. "A thousand shades of blue, a million shades of green!" I call out, our cottage slogan for water and bush. Like everyone we know, we love the Big Lake with passion.

"And a million water diamonds just for us." Mimi ducks and comes up squealing, tossing more water diamonds into the air. "Land of the silver birch, home of the beaver..." she yodels, splashing me hard.

I look around for the doctor and there he is in front of the cottage with a shovel, digging purposefully. He sends us a saluting wave and I wave wildly back with both hands. Out on the road behind the cottage, Regina and Holly are heading for the courts, two white blurs against the greenery, too far to see us.

"Regina is pretty good at tennis, but my sister is terrible," Mimi says. "She misses lots. I think it's her eyes. They'll never get past the first round."

I dare Mimi to swim under the raft and, as usual, she follows my lead. It's black under there and we have to hold our breath for a long time and keep our eyes open so we don't surface too soon and bump our heads on the underside. We stay in the water until we hear the clangs from the iron triangle, the signal to change for lunch.

Inside the screen porch, Mrs. Gordon has laid out a huge spread—cold chicken, hard boiled eggs, coleslaw, potato salad, bits of celery with cheese in them, pound cake and custard, and lots of grapes, my favourite fruit. A pitcher of milk and a pile of bread sit on the table as well.

The doctor talks about the roses, thrillingly addressing most of his remarks to me. The others show no interest in gardening; they are all taken up with the tournament. "I've got the two Hansas in," he says with satisfaction. His khaki pants and shirt are streaked with dirt, but his hands are pinky clean. "Wish I had brought more manure. Bloody lot of stones out there too."

"Garnet," says Mrs. Gordon. "Please."

"What's a Hansa?" I say.

"The world's toughest rose, Janet, an old rugosa from 1905. You've seen them all over town. Our most popular rose. They're the big dark green guys covered with magenta flowers. Lovely rosy scent.

I've put them right under the screens in front of the porch.

"The back steps are for the two Finns. Also known as the White Rose of Finland. The little Scotch rose goes on the side of the porch. They're hardy as hell and tough as nails. They all should do fine except I'm worried about the Scotch. It looks a bit peak-ed. Got dried out a bit, perhaps, so I'm counting on Scottish pluck to bring it through." He waves his beer bottle. "Scotland the brave," he says as he takes a long swig.

Mrs. Gordon raises her eyebrows and sighs gently.

After they all go off to the tournament, Mrs. Gordon and I stay behind to tackle the mountain of lunch dishes, first carrying everything to the back on trays.

"My, my, Janet, you certainly are handy in the kitchen. Your mother has taught you very well," she says in her precise voice. She boils water on the stove for the dishpan while I put several sheets of newspaper on the kitchen table, scrape the scraps into the centre, and carefully fold up the package tying it securely with string. "My girls could learn a lot from you."

We are hanging the tea towels on the clothes line when Regina and Holly burst into the back yard. "We were eliminated," they call out, "just as we thought. But Mimi's doing swell. She's won her first set."

At the courts, we make a line on the bleachers: I beside Mrs. Gordon, then the doctor, Holly and Regina. I try to follow the game, but Mrs. Gordon's

THE ART OF BURGLARY

brief explanations make no sense to me. About a dozen players stand at the mesh partially blocking our view while dogs and little kids chase each other in the grass behind us and a grown-up with an armband and a megaphone calls out instructions. From time to time, everyone claps and cheers, but I'm never sure why. A breeze from the lake swoops in and, far above, puffball clouds sail across the sky.

There are long stretches when Mimi doesn't have to play. However, she doesn't come up to see me but mills around with the others watching the competition and talking to her cottage friends below. Mrs. Gordon also enters into long chats with cottage ladies. I begin to feel restless and left out.

The doctor slips off his perch. "I'll get the last of the digging done. It may rain tomorrow and I want to get that Scotch rose in. Be back later."

After checking her gold watch, Holly turns to her mother. "O.K. Mummsy, two hours are up since lunch so it's safe to swim and so," she and Regina stand up, "we two are disappearsville." They jump down and run along the road towards the cottage.

I think longingly of the pile of movie magazines I saw on the table between the two beds in the mezzanine when Mimi and I carried up our clothes. Would it be possible to run over to the cottage and get a few to read at the tournament between sets? Perhaps I should ask Mrs. Gordon, but she has gone down to the mesh and is deep in chat. After waiting a while, I hop off the bleachers and pelt down the road.

Up on the balcony above the living room, I can hear the doctor's shovel outside the screens. Then

87

Holly comes in, wearing a towel over her bathing suit. Letting the screen door slam, she strides across the porch and the living room, swinging her bathing cap in a circle. Her wet feet make squash noises when they hit the wooden floor in the kitchen and out the back door. She's off to the biffy, no doubt.

I sort through the pile of magazines, carefully putting the best ones on the railing. June Allyson and Van Johnson are my favourite stars. The doctor's shovel stops and I can hear him slapping his hands on his trousers. *Maybe he will come in for a beer*, I think hopefully, *and then maybe talk to me.*

"Inside," I hear him say and I crane my neck to look below into the living room.

Regina, wet from swimming and holding a towel, comes into the porch with him right behind her. She turns and he takes the towel and begins to dry her blond hair. She bends her head forward towards him and laughs in her squeaky way. A second later, he swings one arm around her shoulder and kisses her, actually kisses her, and presses close to her as if he wants to glue himself to her body. His mouth seems to be slobbing all over hers. Even worse, she puts her soggy arms around his neck. They both make yucky noises.

With my head almost squeezed between the bars trying to see everything, I must have jolted the railing because the pile of movie magazines above me slides forward one after another. They drop slowly, in a fluttery flapping way like a slow moving pack of cards. Some of them glide across the varnished floor until they almost touch Regina's feet. She jumps back, takes one look at me, and, in three strides, vanishes in the direction of the kitchen. The back door slams.

The doctor glares at me. "Janet. Jesus Christ," he says. Then he too disappears out the front. In a minute, I hear the chunk of the shovel.

I climb down in a sort of fever. I pick up all the magazines and put them on the little wicker table by the Quebec heater. What to do? I can hear my heart pounding as I pivot this way and that. Should I go and talk to the doctor? Better not. Should I hide upstairs in the mezzanine under the covers until it's time to go home tomorrow? This is what I want to do—just disappear somewhere and think over what I have seen and let the hurt wash over me. Perhaps I should run into the woods across the road and they would all have to come looking for me and, at last, perhaps by sunset, just when everyone has given up hope, the doctor would rescue me and say...and say? My imagination turns as cold as Lake Superior and I know that I am making up a silly dream.

Just as silly as all my dreams, I think bitterly.

Better to go back to the tennis courts and pretend nothing happened. I'll tell Mrs. Gordon I'd gone to the biffy. And that is what I do. I sit on the bleachers in the sun and feel my life unraveling. There's a big cheer when the tournament ends and I try to join in. Mimi comes second in her age group, and eventually, the megaphone says she will get a cup with her name engraved on it. More clapping and a general move homeward.

JOAN BARIL

The evening passes in a numb sort of way. Holly and Regina go off to a wiener roast and Mrs. Gordon sets out a cold ham supper on the porch. The doctor doesn't appear for supper. After we are in bed, some neighbours drop by to play cards and Mimi and I, up in our mezzanine, can hear them talking on the screen porch until late, while the slow northern twilight blues out the world. The waves shushing in the background send Mimi to sleep, but I know I will never sleep again. My heart is an ice lump in my chest and I desperately want to cry. No, I want to howl. Instead I put my fist into my mouth.

Later, I hear Mrs. Gordon say in her soft sighing voice, "Not another one, Garnet, please." The sound of a popping bottle cap follows.

And later again, I hear a tumbling noise and, when I look through the bars, I see their shapes. She's helping him as he stumbles across the room. He bumps against the wicker table with the movie magazines on it, knocking it over.

"I'm all right," he says. "Always all right." He lurches forward. "Scotland the brave," he mutters before he disappears into their bedroom.

Late the next afternoon, Mimi and I sit in the front seat and wave good-bye to Mrs. Gordon. Holly and Regina—who is staying on another week —have gone off somewhere. The back seat of the car is filled with bags of laundry for Scotty to do and the trunk is filled with a carton of garbage and two cases of empty beer bottles. Mimi, who has one more week of school before she moves out to the cottage for the summer, will stay home under

90

the care of Scotty while the doctor is at work. And from then on, he will stay at home alone, coming out only on weekends, like most of the fathers do in families that own cottages.

"If you join us next weekend, I can teach you how to play tennis." Mimi says as the highway hums beneath us. "And swimming lessons are starting. Maybe you can learn the crawl at last. Your swimming is pretty clunky." She leans toward her dad. "Janet can only do the side stroke."

At the wheel, the doctor just grunts. "We'll see," he says, and I know he's mad at me.

❖

"So," my mother says at supper the following Wednesday. "What's this I hear about your behaviour at the Gordon cottage?"

"What?" I say, with a sudden lurch that somehow the whole story has come out.

"The doctor says you were unruly."

"No," I cry. "No, I wasn't." I am emphatic, but I know that this will cut no ice with my mother. "I was very helpful. I did the dishes."

My mother interrupts. "Well, that's it for gallivanting off. You can stay in town on the weekends after this. Tennis! Swimming lessons! What other nonsense are they cooking up down there?"

"I didn't do anything. I was good." But it's useless to argue. As I run out of the house, I yell, "Doctor Gordon is a big fat liar."

Obviously the doctor no longer wants me around. I was once his friend, but now he hates me because I saw him kissing that stupid Regina. So, he tells lies about me. What a jerk, I think, a jerk of the first water. I feel the last remnants of my daydream life ripping away, turning into wisps, and leaving me shamed and alone.

❖

I wait behind the lilacs for Doctor Gordon early the next morning to catch him as he leaves for work. I know Mimi will still be in bed and Scotty will be in the kitchen. In the flowerbed, the Dorion iris is in sunny bloom. When the doctor comes down the front steps carrying his doctor's bag, he immediately walks over to look at it.

"I am not 'ruly!" I yell as I step forward "You told my mother I am 'ruly, but I am not."

"Ah, Janet," he says between his teeth.

"Ask Mrs. Gordon," I yell. "I helped her in the kitchen and she said I was very handy. Just ask her."

Then comes the glance. A glance through narrowed eyes and focused on me. A long considering glance that I do not understand until years later. A glance that is deciding how to go on, even with the threat standing before him.

"I want you to tell my mother I wasn't 'ruly. I have never done a bad thing in life." This is a lie, I realize as it pops out of my mouth. In fact, isn't this lie practically as bad as the one the doctor told my mother? And of course he knows it to be so. The

THE ART OF BURGLARY

glance ends. He makes up his mind, turns, and walks rapidly toward his car.

"Except once," I say, trying to think of something to soften the baldness of the fib. "I did one bad thing. I ate my hair ribbon."

His hand hovers toward the car door.

"You did what?'

"I ate my hair ribbon."

"How long was this hair ribbon?" He walks back towards me.

I hold up my hands about a foot apart.

Now he squats down in front of me, but I can barely see him because big tears are falling out of my eyes. "When did you do this, Janet?"

"Last Christmas," I mumble. "It was a horrible green plaid thing. My mother made me wear it. I didn't want to throw it in the snow so I ate it." I want to add that I was a lot younger then and it seemed like a good idea at the time.

"And did you, Janet, ah...ever see the ribbon again?" He leans toward me.

"No."

"Very interesting," he says. He sits back on his heels.

"That's the truth, Doctor Gordon, but you are a fibber. You can ask Mrs. Gordon if I..."

He dabs at my face with his big soap-smelling handkerchief. "You're right, I am a fibber indeed. And we don't have to bring Mrs. Gordon into this in any way. OK?"

I nod.

"I'll phone your mother today."

I make a big snuffle and, taking the hanky, blow my nose hard, almost not hearing what I was hearing.

"And you come down to the cottage with Mimi this week-end. We'll see about getting some swimming lessons. How about that?"

I nod and stare at my shoes, wondering what has just happened.

"Keep the handkerchief," he says as he gets into the car. "And don't eat it, you hear." I see him laughing as he drives away.

I walk over to the Dorion Gold iris and stare at it. So that's how grown-ups get away with doing bad things, I think. They just admit their fault and drive off. Nothing happens to them. They keep doing what they want. They laugh.

I frown at the iris, thinking hard. If I step on the stem, I can squash it to the ground, then smash the bloom with the other foot. I take a step closer but hesitate. I think of Mimi and the beautiful lake, tennis and swimming lessons, and finally learning to do the crawl.

Nevertheless, I lift my foot and hold it over the plant. But the iris is now wide to the world, too beautiful, too full of life. I kneel beside it and put my face close to its glowing throat. The wavy edges of the big petals touch my cheek. Ziggy magenta veins shimmer in the deep gold interior. I smooth the ribbed falls with my fingertips. A flower is so simple and unafraid, I think, and not like me all twisted up within and the knowledge that, whether I am asked or not, no matter how many times, or

THE ART OF BURGLARY

how much Mimi begs, I'll never go to that cottage ever again.

THE SISTERHOOD

The family secret was slipping out. At sixteen, I reacted with intense embarrassment. I didn't realize that another secret, more intense and more interesting, was also hiding close by.

In 1965, I worked Saturdays at the boys' department in Eaton's. When the closing bell shrilled, my cousin, Midge, who was head of the department, and I began straightening the stacks of sweaters and bush jackets on the wooden counters and covering them with long blue drop cloths. Just to make conversation and because I knew Midge was familiar with the family secret, I said, "I'm going with my mother over to Miss O'Shea's tomorrow afternoon. She lost her engagement ring."

Midge's hands flew to her face and the pile of boys' wool socks she was carrying flipped in a cascading arc. "What in God's name are you talking about, Janet?" She didn't pick up the socks. Instead, she stared at me, one hand on the counter as if for support.

"Miss O'Shea's my algebra teacher," I said.

"I know that," Midge snapped. "What the hell is this about an engagement ring? Surely you are not telling me that Mary Margaret O'Shea is engaged?"

THE ART OF BURGLARY

"Oh, yes," I said, "But she's lost the—"

"Hold your horses," Midge barked, flinging both palms toward me. Then she stooped for the socks, flinging them roughly on the counter. She grabbed the cotton cover that I was holding and flipped it over the merchandise. "I'll organize when I come in on Monday."

I was speechless. Midge was an exacting boss and insisted on a rigid closing-time routine. Everything had to be in order before we left the floor.

"OK, OK," she said, her voice trembling. "This is what we're going to do. I'll take you out for supper. OK? How about a Stan-and-Sy at the Arthur Cafe? Phone your mother and tell her."

I nodded, too surprised to reply. But I loved the gravy-laden hot sandwiches at the café across the street and a Stan-and-Sy was certainly better than the creamed peas on toast waiting at home.

A quarter of an hour later, I was sitting in a booth trying to think of calming words, although I had no idea why my news had so agitated my cousin. "Miss O'Shea came to our house last night," I slowly started in. "She said she'd lost her engagement ring. It's got two diamonds. She's sure it's somewhere in her suite. She says she's never worn it in public yet. She's only been engaged for a week. She said she'd heard about my mother and came for help."

I blushed. My mother's ability to find lost objects made me squirm with mortification. Both my mother and Midge's mother, my Aunt Sissy, had inherited the so-called "Gift." They also saw the future in tea leaves. However, these facts were seldom mentioned outside the family circle. This suited me fine. I cringed to think what the kids at Port Arthur Collegiate would say if they learned my mother was psychic.

But unfortunately, some rumours must have slithered out. Witness Miss O'Shea's visit.

Midge poured the tea from the brown crockery pot. "Did she say who she's engaged to?"

"Mr. Muir, the physics teacher."

"Never heard of him," Midge said. Then she added, "The poor sap."

I could not figure Midge out at all. "I think it's wonderful," I said stoutly. "Now she won't be an old maid any more. She probably thought she'd never get married because she's pretty old."

The waitress lowered the Stan-and-Sy in front of me. It was a six-inch tall layered concoction of white bread, roast pork, and sliced onion awash in thick brown gravy. A two-inch high dike of French fried potatoes circled the edge of the plate. I breathed in the mesmerizing richness of gravy and fat and, leaning over, took up my knife and fork.

Midge was frowning and shaking her head, but she turned to the waitress. "Alma, would you bring me a salt fish sandwich on rye please. And more hot water for the tea."

"Mary Margaret O'Shea is thirty-four," said Midge to me, emphasizing each word. "That is not old Janet. And there are worse things than being an old maid."

"Such as?" I said, shaking vinegar on the fries.

THE ART OF BURGLARY

"Marrying someone you don't love for one thing. Marrying a man, when you're not suited to it. Marrying, so your religious family will be happy and shut up about it. Marrying, because you think it's the right thing to do."

I was indignant. "That's not fair, Midge," I said. "You don't know that."

"Look," said Midge, "do you know the bookkeeper at Eaton's, Elaine Gatherum? She lives with Mary Margaret O'Shea and has done so for the last ten years. How do you think she feels about this engagement?"

I shrugged. I only knew the bookkeeper to say hello and I didn't even know Miss O'Shea very well outside of school. "I think she'd be happy to see her friend married at last," I said.

Midge sighed. She looked at her open-faced sandwich and pushed it away. But then she pulled it back, took several paper serviettes from the holder, wrapped the sandwich carefully, and put it in her purse. "OK, Janet, I'm off. I can't make you see any more than that. I'll pay the bill and you finish up that monstrosity. Do you want Boston Cream Pie for dessert?"

I nodded, taking a big forkful of sandwich. "Oh thank you, Midge," I said. Gravy runnelled down my chin. "This is wonderful."

❖

The next afternoon, as my mother and I walked the two blocks to Miss O'Shea's place, my mother grumbled. "I must be daft Janet. I should 'a said to her right out, 'G'wan with ye, I have nay time for foolishness, losing her ring in her own house. Rank carelessness.' But I'm too polite, I am."

I said nothing, afraid she would turn back. Originally, I had begged to go because I had heard at school that Miss O'Shea's suite was decorated in the new light Scandinavian style and I was dying to see it. My plan, when I married, was to have all light colours in my own place. But it was impossible not to mull over Midge's mysterious hints that had me speculating on the whole affair.

My mother was still grumbling. "Mind, if she pushes university for you again, I'll leave."

I winced. A year ago, when I was in grade eleven, Miss O'Shea had come over to our house one evening to talk about me and suggest I was a good candidate for university. My mother had just laughed and smiled and made tea and set out the scones, but later she rounded on me. "What is it with you? This is the second teacher planting ideas in your head." My grade eight teacher, Miss Joliette, also had mentioned university one time when she met my mother on the street. "You attract all these old biddies. A bright lass you are indeed. University! Huh! Who pays for that, eh?"

Before we could knock, Miss O'Shea opened the door of her third floor suite. She must have heard us coming up the stairs. "Oh, so good of you to come, Mrs. Marsden," she said. Her eyes were puffed into slits behind her glasses and her face was so splotched she looked like a spotted apple. Her reddish hair stuck up around her head like a caragana bush in a high wind.

Arms out, she swooped toward us, capturing both my mother's hands in hers. She held them up as if they were precious objects and rocked them back and forth. My mother's face fell into astonished stone. For a dreadful second, I thought Miss O'Shea was going to clutch my mother's hands to her rounded bosom or, even worse, fling her arms around my mother and cry on her shoulder. It would be the end of the visit, I knew. We would be out the door and down the stairs, and I would hear about nothing else for weeks.

"Oh, so good, so good to help me, Mrs. Marsden." She rocked. Every word had a little sobbing stutter in it. "I've searched everywhere. I can't look any more, I can't do it..." Her lip quivered as if she were gasping for air.

I couldn't look at her. I'd never seen a teacher cry before; I felt my toes curdle. My mother snatched away her hands. Even though I knew my mother wanted to say, "Don't blether, for heaven's sake," she pasted on a ghastly smile. "Shall we make a start?" she said through clenched teeth.

"Of course, of course." Miss O'Shea took a hanky from her sleeve and wiped her eyes. She indicated the way into the living room. "I put those things out." A small velvet box and a picture of a ring cut from the Eaton's catalogue sat on the pale plastic coffee table. "Maybe they will help." Her voice snuffled, but she was trying hard for a smile. "Janet, would you like a glass of milk? Should I put the kettle on? To read the tea leaves perhaps?"

My mother shook her head, and sat down on the grey sofa, first pushing away some towels that were tumbled there. She put her purse on the floor beside her. She picked up the blue velvet case, opened it and stared at the empty interior, snapped it closed and turned it round and round in her hand. She looked down at the small paper with the picture of the ring, but did not pick it up.

"I never wore it," Miss O'Shea faltered. "Not once. I never took it outside. It must be in here somewhere. I've looked..."

"Do shush," said my mother, "and sit down."

Miss O'Shea sat.

I was so nervous of my mother's temper I could not enjoy the Scandinavian living room. For one thing, it was a mess. Half the books in the beige wooden bookcase were spilled out on the floor or piled on the grey carpet. On the pink walls, here and there, were lighter coloured squares, as if someone had removed the pictures. Even the pale grey easy chairs and sofa with their wooden arms were littered in clothes which we had to push aside to sit down. More piles of clothes were on the plastic end tables. On the table beside me, the pink ceramic heads of two flamingos poked through a jumble of rayon underpants. *Teacher underpants!* I did not know which way to look.

I wanted to ask many questions, but I dared not open my mouth. I knew my mother would shush me as sharply as she had shushed the algebra teacher. *Nancy Drew was never told to shush*, I raged inwardly. Neither was Miss Marple. They could ask questions whenever they wanted. For example, where was Miss Gatherum, the jealous roommate? Did my mother even know she existed?

102

THE ART OF BURGLARY

Had the bookkeeper grabbed all her stuff and books and pictures and stormed away, green-eyed and frothing over Miss O'Shea's good luck at catching a man? Obviously, the roommate was the culprit. She could have taken the ring and disposed of it anywhere. Flushed it down the toilet. Tossed it out the window into the snow. Taken it to Eaton's and hid it among the merchandise for a lucky customer to find.

"Uh huh," my mother said. Whenever my mother attempted to locate a lost object, she did not go into a trance or sway back and forth or do any kind of fortune teller routine. She just sat and, as she often told me, the idea would come, or it would not. I had once overheard her say to my Aunt Sissy, "We're both a wee bit fey, Sissy, 'tis true, but we have nay idea where it comes from for a' that. Thank God our girls have not inherited the Gift."

Now my mother stood up abruptly and headed for the front hall. Miss O'Shea and I immediately followed. "You're right. It's in this suite somewhere." She reached into the closet and, taking out my coat, tossed it to me and then took down her own. Over her shoulder she said, "It could be in the kitchen." She opened the front door and sat on the top step to put on her overshoes. I waited behind her until she had finished.

Miss O'Shea seemed unable to speak, but she followed the retreating back down the stairs. "But I've looked, I've looked," she called. "I can't look any more..."

A few steps down, my mother turned and I thought I saw some sort of expression on her face.

Was it possible it was sympathy? "Our Janet will stay and help you then," she said.

"What, me?" I cried. My mother shot me a glare as she disappeared around the bend in the stairs. I yanked off the overshoe that I'd been pulling on and stood.

Miss O'Shea opened the kitchen door and beckoned me forward. Piles of dishes took up most of the table. I scanned the room. Every cupboard door and drawer stood open. The counter was covered with pots and cooking gear. What a hodgepodge. But first things first. I must ask my questions, discreetly of course, in good Jane Marple fashion. But, instead it all came out in a big blurt. "Where is Miss Gatherum anyway? She probably snaffled the ring. Out of spite, no doubt."

Miss O'Shea did not answer. She walked to the window and looked out at the snow-covered world below. "She's gone Janet, OK? That's all I know. I haven't a clue where she is. She has an aunt in Winnipeg and she might've gone there, but I don't know. Her car's gone too. And she put the ring case on the coffee table, just as you and your mother saw it. Empty." I opened my mouth, but she headed off my next remark. "And no, I don't think she took it with her. I know her very well. She's the kindest, most loving person. Anyway, your mother said it's around here somewhere, so..."

She turned from the window, her eyes hard and bleak. "But that's not the problem, Janet. The problem is Tom Muir. He suspects, well he has heard, well he suspects a lot of things. When Elaine left, I couldn't see him; I haven't seen him for days.

THE ART OF BURGLARY

He probably thinks... Hell, I don't know what he thinks and I don't care right now. But if I don't wear the ring, you see, and make it public..."

I didn't understand at all. "What? What will happen?"

"If I don't make it public, I might change my mind and I don't want to do that."

"Oh," I said.

Miss O'Shea sat down, shoulders slumped. "My good friends are mad at me for what I'm doing. We're like a sisterhood, and in this small town we stick together. We have to. It's a bit like a family; we're so loyal to each other. All my friends knew I loved Elaine, and I did love her. You have to understand. Sometimes women do. So, the sisterhood feels, oh I don't know if I can explain, but they feel sad. Yes, I think they feel a bit sad about it."

"Oh," I said again. I knew I was learning something important, something grown-up, but I was not sure what. My cousin, Midge, would explain, I thought. Midge knows everything. I'll leave the questions for her.

"Right," Miss O'Shea sighed. "Let's get on with it, shall we? You search the Frigidaire, Janet. I haven't looked in there yet."

I looked at the fridge. "It's not in there," I said. With these words, a soft tremor passed through me, like a shiver of wind on snow. "And it's not in the cupboards either," I went on. "And I don't think it's anywhere on the counter." I looked around. "The drawers maybe..." The tremor intensified into an itch inside my chest, a sort of light interior tickle. I

105

glanced at the line of open drawers and picked the nearest one. It was full of cookbooks. "It's in here somewhere," I said.

I began to pull the books out one at a time. Out of the corner of my eye, I saw Miss O'Shea's head jerk forward and her mouth fall open, but I paid no attention. I was almost there. It was close at hand. I shook each book over the counter: *Joy of Cooking*, *The Five Roses Cookbook*, *Kate Aitken's Canadian Cookbook*, *Fanny Farmer*. As I was doing this, I was also dimly aware of noises far away, a clattering on the stairs and voices.

Under the *Fanny Farmer* was a thick pocket book. *The Well of Loneliness*. Not a cookbook, surely, with a title like that. I shook it hard, but no ring fell out. I had glimpsed a dark shadow among the pages, so I turned the book over in my hand and let it fall open. It parted in the middle section. A neat cube had been cut into the pages in the centre of the book. The ring was there, as I knew it would be, Scotch-taped down inside its paper container. A paper well, I realized, and for Miss Gatherum, a well of loneliness indeed. How sad. I turned to Miss O'Shea, but she was not in the room.

As I stared at the twinkling thing, it winked back at me with a tiny flick of light. "See, you found me after all," it seemed to say. "I knew you would."

The shimmery feeling in my gut was floating away now, replaced by flat-out panic. I vaguely heard voices and laughter coming from the hall, but my brain was in full spin. I knew what had taken place and it wasn't welcome. I had caught the family disease. The psychic ability to find things.

THE ART OF BURGLARY

The hereditary ailment that ran through the generations. The so-called "Gift." Oh God, I was fey. No way. No bloody way was I going to give in to a life of tea leaves and needy people. It was fine for some creepy cottage in Scotland but not in Canada. "This is the new world over here," I said sternly to the rapidly diminishing part of my consciousness. "No weird voices and hocus-pocus for me, thank you very much."

Out loud, I whispered firmly, "Bugger off."

At that minute, I knew I had to get outside, get away from the noxious ring and the vague feeling of triumph for finding it. I rushed out to the hall, but it was full of women, and surprisingly, among them was Midge. "Janet," she said. "We hear you're helping out. And we are too."

She introduced me to the others, but I could not grasp the names. I recognized Miss Joliette, my old Grade Eight teacher, and Miss Treloar who gave private music lessons at people's houses. Old Mrs. Hutchin, my Latin teacher, was there too. I was grappling with my coat and, at the same time, moving toward the door when I saw Miss O'Shea. Her face looked rosy now and happier. It was as if her life had turned around. I pushed the book into her hands. "It's in here," I said. From the babble around me I overheard the words "Elaine" and "Winnipeg."

A minute later, I was running down the stairs, my overshoes flapping. I did not stop until I hit the cold winter air.

I told no one about my newly discovered and unwelcome mystical gift. I simply mentioned to my mother that the ring had been found in the apartment, as she had foretold. Her reply was a grunt.

The following Friday evening at work in Eaton's, I tried to ask Midge a few questions about the Sisterhood, but she was not forthcoming. Like my mother, she gave a sort of grunt. "Huh," she said. "Mary Margaret O'Shea," she sighed, drawling out the name. "The brains of a moth. But she's our friend, so we'll stick by her, I suppose."

She handed me the bottle of lemon oil and set me polishing the varnished counters. "And I'm not going to be a bridesmaid, Janet, if that's what you want to know. And none of our gang is either. I told her to get some of those O'Shea cousins. God knows there are a lot of them. It'll be hard enough to get through the damned wedding, not to mention all the bridal showers they're lining up."

So, a happy ending after all. It was a satisfying thought. Miss O'Shea had not changed her mind about getting married. In fact, plans for the wedding were underway. Wonderful news. I almost mentioned this out loud to Midge, but something stopped me.

I decided, on balance, it would be better to keep silent.

THE RULES OF REVENGE 1952

I was sixteen years old and I was trying to define revenge. Revenge should be elegant, I decided, like Bubsie's revenge on her boyfriend. Bubsie, who was my cousin Midge's best friend, had devised a plot so diabolical and so clever, it was a masterpiece. It was not criminal in any way, but did what revenge was supposed to do: give joy to the giver and pain to the receiver.

At heart, I reasoned, revenge was transformation. It takes the pain away from me and puts it elsewhere. Where it belongs.

In the days following Christmas, the desire for revenge engulfed my belly and brain like hot lava. My target was the Roman Catholic Church.

Christmas afternoon and the whole family was sitting down in our living room for the big dinner. The furniture had been pushed back to make room for the table, my mother and Aunt Sissy had taken their aprons off and my father, who was a policeman and had just come off shift, had changed out of his uniform.

JOAN BARIL

"Will the youngest say grace?" my Uncle Everett said. My sister flashed her dimples and started in. Saying grace was a once-a-year Christmas event in our house. I tried to look pious while my cousin Midge, who had begun to eat, tried to look pious with her mouth full.

The front door bell rang and I went to answer it. It was Joe St. Onge, president of St. Martin's Young People's Club. I did not know him well and he didn't seem to recognize me at all. He was a jowly young man of about twenty in a heavy mackinaw. His eyes were popping under the peak of his bush cap as if searching for help. His jaw hung open, but then it always did.

"Hi," I said.

"Are you uh—are you uh—Janet?"

"Yes."

"I've been asked to tell you...I mean it has been decided..."

With one hand on the door knob, I leaned forward to catch the words that seemed to be hiding behind the white plume of ice breath emerging from his mouth. He shuffled a couple of inches backward as if he were going to flee.

"We don't want you to come to the Youth Centre any more or have anything to do with the Young People's Club. It's for church members only."

Had I really heard that? His words did not fit together. They fluttered about my ears like snowflakes. "What!" I snapped, intending to demand what was going on.

A hand appeared over my shoulder. "That's fine," my mother said, closing the door. "Come and get

110

your dinner, Janet. You can't stand here with the door open wasting the heat."

I ate like a zombie. I knew I had done nothing untoward and there was no reason to be treated so, to be banished from the centre of my social life and possibly severed from all my friends. The pain of the injustice burned at my insides. I excused myself and went upstairs to lie down.

The next day, I told my mother, but she said what I expected. "I canna ken these religious folk. You're nay Catholic so they dinna want you. Ye'll not set yer foot where it's not welcome, so that's the all of it."

But that evening, my thoughts swerved to revenge and stayed there.

I discovered Bubsie's vengeance by accident. I was often sent on errands to my Aunt Sissy's a few blocks away and one Friday, just as I was leaving her house, my cousin Midge sidled up to me with a paper bag in her hand.

"Can you stop at Bubsie's on your way home?" she said. "She needs this for a project she's working on."

On the street, I peeked. Inside was a single tea bag.

Bubsie was a lucky person. She had a good job at Simpson's as head of the bookkeeping department, a handsome boyfriend named Leo, and most importantly, her own suite, four small rooms in an old house on Jean Street. I envied her a great deal.

No one answered my knock, so I pushed open the unlocked door of the apartment, intending to leave the mysterious bag in the kitchen. The table was covered with sheets of paper crinkled up at the edges and coated with a grainy substance. I could make out faint words underneath penned in a rounded script.

"Your velvet thighs," I read out loud. "The eye of paradise, the flower of the flame." I was puzzling out some more when Bubsie came in. She must have been working late, for she was wearing her navy crepe dress and her hair was up in a chignon.

"From Midge," I said, handing her the bag.

She looked inside. "Great. I didn't want to buy a whole box of tea for one bag."

I looked at the table in a mute question.

"Yeah, well, Leo's coming over for—uh— breakfast tomorrow and I'm going to serve him up his so-called poetry. "

"Oh?" I said.

"Leo's been stepping out on me, the rat. So I've taken his dim-witted poetry, which he always gives me instead of anything that costs money, and I've dipped the pages in boiled sugar water and I'm going to tear them up in teeny tiny bits and serve them to him mixed with his cornflakes. The two-timing cheapskate is going to eat his own words."

Genius. "But why the tea bag?"

"For colour. The way the sheets are now, they don't look brown enough to pass as cornflakes. I'm going to dip them again."

She gave me a glass of milk and I watched as she put water in a frying pan, tossed in some sugar and

THE ART OF BURGLARY

the tea bag and set it to boil. "Here's some advice for you, Janet. Never go steady with a handsome man. They're all conceited. Find a nice guy who's ugly. Also someone who's not tight with money."

As I went down the stairs of the apartment house, I marvelled at the brain that could conceive such a brilliant plan. No wonder they'd made her head of the bookkeeping department. Still, I had never heard of anyone coming to visit for breakfast. It seemed an odd time of day for a date.

Three days after Christmas with the lava still smouldering in my gut, I got up early, put on my long woollen coat and kerchief and walked down the hill to St. Martin's. My intention was to check out the place before anyone was around. I wanted to find something to destroy.

But I had not counted on Catholic piety. The church contained many praying people, some lighting candles at the shrines and others lining up before a confessional. As well, the outer porch and back wall were covered with scaffolding and workmen. I tried a wobbly genuflection, as I had seen my Catholic friends do, and sat down in a pew to look around and think the situation over.

Shortly after I started high school, four years earlier, I went with my neighbourhood friend, Alena Charlotte, to St. Martin's Youth Centre, which had recently opened in the church basement. On the corner, we'd met three girls, friends of Alena Charlotte's from Catholic Elementary.

"Are you sure I'm allowed in?" I asked the group after the introductions. I didn't know if they let a non-Catholic take part in the church activities.

"No problem. Besides, you can bowl can't you?" said Teresa, a stout redhead with a bossy face.

"Only once."

"That's once more than any of us," said Teresa. "We're signing up now before all the spots are gone." She hustled us down the steps where two bowling alleys and three new pool tables had taken over the church basement.

We became the Hot Pepper Bowling Team, but, to each other, we became "the gang"—best friends for life. As for the Young People's Club, which started up about the same time, I assumed I could not be a member, but I felt welcome at the events held in the church hall. The Valentine Tea, amateur night, the Hallowe'en Hop, the Saturday night dances with the Bob Schaefer band or the Roma Boogie-Woogie Combo—I attended them all.

In the spicy-smelling church, I closed my eyes and thought about Alena Charlotte's twin brother Artie, so handsome in his gabardine strides, jive dancing with me, my black suede baby doll shoes flashing on the hardwood floor, the saxophone swirling around us. Gone. The church had power, I knew. As well as banning me from the Youth Centre and the Young People's Club, would the Hot Pepper Gang and Artie be advised to avoid me? Would I still be on the bowling team? The candles flickering

THE ART OF BURGLARY

in front of the statue of the Blessed Virgin blurred into a mist. *Mary*, I prayed, *you are the patron of women—or at least I think you are. So help me now, please. Don't let me lose my friends. And give me one idea, one good idea, to get even. Amen.*

A little door at the side popped open and Father Fry rushed in, cassock fluttering. He made a sweeping genuflection before the altar, then flung himself onto a small kneeling bench at the side. He stretched his arms full out, tossed his head back and closed his eyes.

Two months before I had been in the kitchen of the church hall helping with the preparations for the Sock Hop when Father Fry had appeared, clapping his hands loudly. "Stop what you are doing, everyone. We must take time for the blessed rosary." I stayed in the back, very still with my head bowed, as everyone around me made their responses.

Had this incident led to my dismissal? Had he seen me and demanded to know who I was? Had he found out I wasn't a Catholic? I cringed to think there has been some sort of meeting, perhaps with the entire executive, and that I had been discussed. It was worse than getting your name in the newspapers.

I shot eye daggers at my enemy who was swaying slightly on the kneeler. I could easily hit him with a spitball at this distance, or I could walk forward and, when I got close, lurch sideways and knock him off his perch. On the other hand, if I had a container, I could get holy water and pour it down the neck of his cassock. Interesting

115

daydreams took over, but I snapped out of it. So childish. I was too young for this game, I realized. Not old and clever like Bubsie.

On the other hand, maybe I could slip down into the Youth Centre and rip up the green baize on the pool tables with the nail scissors in my purse. But that would be a criminal act and break my own rules. Besides, it might lead to horrible consequences. Basically, I was too chicken to do it.

I dried my eyes with the ends of my kerchief and scuttled out of the church, colliding in the porch with a leg of the scaffolding. "Hey," a workman called down. He was holding a large painting in his hands and his mate was hammering a nail into the plaster. Below, more paintings were leaning against the wall. A well-placed kick should send them flying, I thought. I readied my right foot, swinging it slightly to warm it up, but several people came in at that minute and my nerve failed again. I dashed out.

On Monday morning, the first day of school after Christmas, I scuffed through the snow clods with a pile of binders and textbooks cradled to my chest. The front door of Alena Charlotte's house burst open and she came flying out so fast her modern history text flipped into the snow.

"Janet, look what I got." Her coat was open at the top to show the pale pink of an Orlon Kitten sweater underneath.

"Lucky duck," I said, snatching up her book and flapping it to clear the flakes. At the same time, the pain in my gut was sailing off like a winter bird and then dissolving into the heavens as I spied the rest

THE ART OF BURGLARY

of the gang on the corner waving at us. *Oh thank you, Blessed Mary, thank you.* I still had my friends.

We compared Christmas presents right up to the door of history class where Teresa said, "Don't forget, Hot Peppers, bowling starts this Friday."

Was that possible? In class, my soul soared to the ceiling and Mr. Severage, with his pointer and map of Europe, floated with it. I giggled out loud in sheer giddiness.

"Miss Marsden." He fixed me with narrowed eyes. "I note with some surprise that you find the assassination of the Czar amusing."

"No, Sir."

"The entire royal family is gunned down, and you titter like a mating gull."

The class guffawed. "Sorry, sir."

"Tomorrow, we will discuss the reaction of the Western Powers to the Communist take-over of Russia. I hope, Miss Marsden, you will arrive sober?"

"Yes, sir." The class was roaring with laughter, but I did not care. I wafted from the room.

❖

After school, my mother sent me down to Eaton's for basting thread and a new darning egg. I slipped a quarter into my mitt with the intention of stopping at St. Martin's and putting it in the little box at the foot of the Virgin. But just as I turned up the wide church walk, Father Fry came out talking animatedly with a younger priest. I shrank into the shadows of a high snow bank.

After my purchases, I headed for Midge's counter in the children's department. I loved my cousin a lot. I loved her high energy, her warm nature, and her quick and practical mind. All the family relied on her. And I knew she was an excellent sales woman. A bit stout, yes, but with a beautiful round face and a halo of curly brown hair. She was folding up for the day, piling romper suits into the glass cases. She smiled when she saw me. "I have a question for you," she said.

"And I have a question for you. Did Leo eat the cereal? I'm dying to know."

She shook her head. "Uh-uh Janet, I'm not talking about that. Big, fat, dark secret. But since you're involved, go and ask her yourself. She'll be getting home from work pretty soon."

Twenty minutes later I was at Bubsie's door.

"Janet," she cried out in welcome, hugging me and even kissing me on both cheeks. Her Tabu perfume set me reeling with pleasure. Over tea, we beamed at each other across the spotless kitchen table. No tea-stained poetry in sight.

"It worked like a charm, Janet, "Bubsie said, still smiling. Leo didn't notice a damn thing. I gave him good coffee and a big pile of rye toast. Also, I wore my new red peignoir." I must have looked puzzled.

"Distraction, Janet," she said. "Sheer distraction."

"But did you tell him he was eating his own poetry?"

"Of course. At first he thought I was joking and then he started to yell. He said I had snatched the living heart out of his bosom and ripped it into bloody shreds."

THE ART OF BURGLARY

"Oh, come on," I said

"He is a bit melodramatic," she said. "Here's some advice for you Janet. Men are like cigarettes; you can get hooked very easily."

I laughed.

"I was all ready to swear off the habit forever, but..." She raised her fine eyebrows.

"But what? Don't tell me you went back to him?" I couldn't believe it.

"Well, he whined so beautifully. And it was Christmas. And the New Year's Eve formal was coming up. I let him sweat a couple of days. Then I made him swear in writing that he'd never chase another skirt. Besides, he always made copies of the poems. I knew that, so they weren't really lost.

"So, yeah, we're a duo again. But the basic fact is this. He's scared stiff I'll tell his buddies about eating his own words." She smiled a sneaky, close-lipped smile. "So, I swore I wouldn't. You and Midge are the only ones who know."

She paused. "For now," she said.

"Right," I said, my brain in a spin. "I haven't told anyone." I crossed my heart over my woollen coat. "And I never will."

She just smiled.

That night Midge phoned. "Do you want a job, Janet? We're going to stay open Friday nights from now on and Saturdays afternoons are picking up too. I thought of you right away. You can't be making much babysitting."

Friday night—bowling night. But hadn't I always known, in the sensible corner of my mind, it was impossible? How could I go bowling and, at the same time, be looking out for Father Fry or Joe St. Onge or someone else on the executive? How could I have any fun if I were worried I'd be turfed out any minute? Midge's offer gave me an out, an excuse to resign from the Hot Peppers. I swallowed hard as a searing depression took over. "Great," I said. "Thank you, Midge."

"The manager and I are good friends," she said. I already put a word in. Come back tomorrow and I'll take you to see her. Wear your blue dress."

When I put down the phone, I felt as if I had been pushed off a cliff and could never climb back. Still, I reminded myself, there was a sliver of brightness. I had a job, I'd have more money and it would be interesting to work with Midge. She could teach me a lot.

The next day, after a promising meeting with the manager, I realized I still had the quarter in my mitt, but no way was I going to give it to the Virgin Mary. True, I still had my girlfriends, but I had lost a lot of my social life. Yet something drew me up the church steps, perhaps the solace of the stained glass light on the snow, or the remembrance of the soft smile on the face of the Virgin. My overshoes, on their own accord, walked me towards the carved wooden door.

The porch inside was blocked by an elderly couple looking up a ladder where a young priest balanced precariously, holding a large oil painting by the top of its wooden frame. Beside the ladder was the scaffolding and, high up on the third stage, was a workman who appeared to be fixing a small light to the wall.

The priest was tilting the picture so that that it could be seen from below. "Some people believe St. Martin is just as effective at granting requests as St. Anthony," he said.

The elderly woman nodded. "Is that right, Father?"

"A saint of great piety. Prayers to him have helped in many hopeless cases."

I studied the portrait. It depicted the head and shoulders of an elderly gent whose large beard covered the lower half of the canvas. No halo or hands. In a vague way, it reminded me of someone, perhaps a photo in my history text, someone connected with the Russian Revolution. The faint resemblance to a historical personage hovered above my thoughts like a faint light and then the images coalesced. A wicked idea shot into my brain.

"A fine painting, a wonderful gift, arriving from Italy just when we have the scaffolding to place it high in the porch."

The workman, who had been kneeling to align the light fixture, straightened his back. "All ready, Father," the man called down.

The old couple murmured something and hurried into the church.

Holding the painting in one hand, the priest turned and, grasping a higher rung, took a step up lifting the picture towards the workman who leaned out to take it.

"Oh no," I cried, "You can't put that up."

The priest stopped, the painting held upward. "And why not?"

"It's a trick, a hoax. That is not St. Martin."

"Who is it then?"

"Why, it's a portrait of Karl Marx," I said.

As the picture fell, it twisted, hitting a protruding piece of scaffolding with a satisfying tearing sound. It somersaulted in mid-air and slammed into a board on the lower staging, bounced backwards and hit the marble floor with a gratifying splat. Bits of the wooden frame scattered in a splintering starburst.

"Just as well, really, isn't it? " I said.

The big door gave a pleasant thud behind me.

MR. JOHN ELLIS

"Is it over?" I asked my father when he walked in the house after work. It was April 23, 1953 and I was 18 years old, teaching Grade 2 at Oliver Road School and living at home.

"Shh," my mother whispered to me. "Be quiet. Of course, it's over. It was on the radio."

My father's face was grey as he closed the front door. The first thing he did was remove the lead truncheon and the handcuffs from the pockets of his dark blue mackinaw, setting them, as usual, on the seat of the chair near the door. Next, he took off the mackinaw and carefully placed it over the back of the chair, and after unbuttoning his navy-blue police tunic, added it to the pile. His peaked hat usually topped the lot, but, after he set it in place, it slid to the floor. He didn't seem to notice, so I picked it up, brushed the flat top, and put it in the usual spot.

I couldn't silence my questions. "Did you meet him?" I asked. For some macabre reason, I was interested in this strange man whose real name was Camille Branchard, but who always used the pseudonym John Ellis when he came to town for a hanging.

My father took the cup of tea handed to him by my mother and settled into his favourite armchair, placing the cup and saucer on the end table beside him. "Not really," he said. "My job was just to stand by as witness, and afterwards, see poor dead Mr. Hlady bundled up and taken off to the cemetery. This cup of tea is the best thing that has happened to me all day. I hope to God I never have to go through that again."

"Would you take a bit of dinner?" My mother said. "It's fish and scalloped potatoes."

My father shook his head, as I knew he would. My mother had told me that after my father had witnessed a hanging a few years back, he couldn't eat for two days. She went into the kitchen and I took the opportunity to ask some questions.

"Was it really horrible?"

"It was fast, Janet. John Ellis does a quick job, that's one thing. Ten seconds and it's over. He carries his own rope in a suitcase when he comes to town. Weighs the man so he can get the right length."

"Why a certain length?"

"If it's too long it takes too long and if it's too short it can rip the head right off the fellow."

A mental picture flashed through my mind. For the first time, I felt the reality, the ghastly reality, of what we were talking about.

My father was going on. "You know Janet, Mr. Ellis is proud of what he does, believes he's doing the right thing, upholding the law and so on." He sighed and shook his head, as if he could not understand it.

THE ART OF BURGLARY

"Does Mr. Ellis really wear a hood when he walks to the scaffold with the condemned man?

"Nay, Janet. That's for the movies."

"But the judge who sentenced him wore a black cap," I said.

"Since you're of an age and so interested," said my dad, "I'll tell you that judges in Canada do not wear black caps. The only person who wore a hood was poor Mr. Hlady himself, so no one could see his face as he stood on the trap. It's as if he's not a real person, hooded like that, like some kind of animal.

"Did he have any last words?" I said undeterred.

"Not that I heard, but me and Sergeant McQueen were standing well back from the gallows."

I opened my mouth to ask another question. I wanted to know what it was like afterwards when, as a witness, my father had to look at the unhooded face, but he held up his hand before I could speak.

"I'll only tell you this. It's wrong, Janet. Wrong to kill a man no matter what he's done. I hope to God this is the last hanging in Port Arthur. You're young and maybe you'll see the law changed because, in the name of God, it is wrong, wrong, wrong."

After that I said nothing.

PART TWO

STILL LIFE WITH BABY

I hold baby Lucia up to the front window as the snow blower turns between the drifts. Her solid body twists, squirms, sways. She's almost two and heavy. I have to brace myself with both legs wide and hold her tight, my head back, ready in case she flips her body backward throwing the hard nut of her skull against my face.

Red and blue flashes light up the morning. The grind shakes the building. A transparent sail lifts, flares, opens against the dark, drifts down in front of the window of our basement apartment. It's January, 1960, and we are half mast in snow. Many days, the same machine returns later in the afternoon. Sometimes, the sidewalk plough comes as well. I start listening for the sounds after our nap.

Should I phone? The question takes up breakfast, the dressing, the first burst of housework. I roll out the wringer washer in the spare bedroom.

"Should I phone?" I ask Lucia, as I cuddle her before putting her in her high chair to keep her away from the washing machine, a rolling canister of scalding water. I load the diapers, watching her from around the corner. She always kills the slices

127

of banana on her tray with her fist before scooping them into her mouth.

As usual, I phone.

Lily arrives just after ten as I'm emptying the machine in the drain in the corner. Her twins, Rex and Nigel, three years and fast, shove past me. Rex carries a metal toy truck as long as his arm. Lily has her Black Cat cigarettes out before I plug the kettle in. She's an Englishwoman with a soft round face and a long upper lip that swoops in from the corners of her mouth to form perfect arcs, never completely concealing her large front teeth. Her lower lip is a lipstick plum. Four years ago, she met Sergeant René Simard, First Battalion, Royal 22 Regiment, on the London Tube when it stopped suddenly and she fell backward into his khaki lap. A week after the wedding at St. Cyprian's in the East End, they moved to the Canadian army base in Germany. She had the twins a year later.

"Bloody rough all round." Lily's red mouth curls downward. "The day after I gave birth, they got me out of bed to mop the floor. Even the officers' wives had to do it. Having kids in Germany is no stroll in the park." She takes a deep drag and pulls my only ashtray close. "When I get preggers again, I'll have it here in Quebec City at St. Joseph de Bellevue." She flips back her long brown hair. "Let the nuns take care of me."

The noise of the twins revving their toy truck up and down the hall crosses her words.

Her eyes slip around my kitchen. "You do keep everything so nice, Janet," she says. "It's too bad you didn't take the apartment upstairs next to mine. It's

THE ART OF BURGLARY

much brighter up there. You wouldn't need the lights on all day like you're in the bottom of a fish bowl. My place is great. If they offer us a house on the army base, I told René not to take it. They group the houses by rank. And I can't stand the thought of some snot officer traipsing through my things, inspecting my housekeeping, taking notes."

She flicks her ash. Perhaps she does not remember that my husband is one of those, 'snot officers.'

I hand Lucia her Raggedy Ann. She tosses it from the highchair. I pick it up and give it to her again. She swings it by one leg in a circle over her head. I pour Lily her tea. "But it's so much cheaper living on the base," I say. "And you get an entire house with a bit of backyard. Besides, it's closer for the men."

She considers this. I can hear the twin's footsteps roaming the apartment. The television in the living room snaps on, emitting a scratchy hum. There are no programs in the morning. The toilet flushes. I hope they've not thrown something in.

"My man comes home every night for supper," Lily says. "He doesn't need to live on the base. Last night, he made chili—first I've ever tasted. Not a bad nosh with a small steak. Not bad at all. The boys tossed theirs down and asked for more. And he helps me get the place to rights. I never get a minute for housework with those two lads."

A stealthy creak. Are they going into my bedroom? I get up to check, but they are hunkered in the dim hall, heads together like two gnomes playing dice. I fill Lucia's cup with milk and tuck Raggedy Ann in beside her.

A long scraping sound like a fingernail on cloth, then a scuffling wail. Lily sighs, places her teacup in the saucer. In a couple of strides she has each boy by the armpit. "Ta, Janet. Lovely tea." I hold the door open for her. Nigel writhes like fish on a line. Rex swings the truck at his brother but slams his mother across the thighs instead. She does not seem to notice. She lifts them out the door and up the stairs.

I turn back to see a long white line, at twin height, streaking the length of the hall, a gouge slashed through the paint and into the drywall, a wave of white on the grey. I put my hand into the crevice, running it along, feeling the ragged paper edges.

Lucia is alone in her high chair. I take her out, change her, all the time talking about the gouge. "Can it be fixed Lucia? What do you think?" I get her snowsuit out of the closet, lay it on the floor and zip it around her. "Will it cost a lot?" Her legs buckle as I push on her snow boots. I put on my jacket and pull my plastic rain boots over my shoes.

Outside the back door, a white sun lights up the bulging clouds. I dig out the big piece of cardboard I stash behind the garbage cans. At the back of the parking area, a drift curves upwards towards the milky sky. I carry the snowsuit bundle that is Lucia to the top, sit her on the cardboard and push it forward, half sliding myself, holding her as she slips down into the snow of the lawn. She squeals and raises her mittened hands for more.

THE ART OF BURGLARY

When my arms begin to buckle, I brush both of us off and place her in the baby sleigh to pull her between the walls of snow to the depanneur on Chemin Ste Foy. The metal runners slice through the new snow on the sidewalk with a shushing sound. I ponder the selection in the meat case for a long time, holding on to Lucia by the top of her hood. "Should I spend the money for a newspaper?" I ask her out loud and look up in confusion to see the owner's dark eyes staring at me under their heavy brows.

"Two pork chops," I say quickly. I decide that if Paul comes home for dinner, I'll cook both for him. Lucia and I will have eggs. If he's late, we'll eat the chops ourselves. Paul eats only meat and potatoes with canned peas. Canned peas are his only vegetable. I put two apples on the counter and add the newspaper. There's still a week to go before my army cheque arrives.

Lunch for Lucia is leftover meatloaf and a cut up tomato. She and I split one of the apples, peeled and chopped into cubes. We nap together on my bed, she between me and the wall. I place one hand on her puffy warm back and drift off to her snuffly baby breathing. Later, I fold the clean diapers in front of the TV. The programming starts at four. Lucia crawls around on an old quilt on the hardwood, occasionally looking at the French cartoons. Neither the sidewalk plough nor the snow blower appears even though it has started snowing again. For supper, we each eat a pork chop and a boiled potato. I show her how to eat with a spoon from a bowl, but she gravely takes out the

131

peas one by one and squashes them with her forefinger. After her bath, I sit with her on the couch, the television sound off, until she falls asleep. I do the dishes, sweep the floor and iron an army shirt for Paul for the next day. I take out the French text and study the next section.

He arrives after eleven. "Long day," he says as he undresses in the lamp's light. "Budgets all day." He's the adjutant of the Second Battalion, Royal Vingt-Deuxieme Regiment, the famous Van Doos. Wasn't it budgets last week? He climbs in and snuggles beside me. I can smell snow on his hair and warm sweat lifting from his body in his sleep.

"What the hell?" It's morning and Paul's fingers are tracing along the gouge in the wall as mine had the day before.

"The Simard twins were here with a metal truck," I say.

"Jesus, what monsters. Never mind, Janet. We'll get some Polyfilla and paint over it somehow."

I do not phone Lily after he leaves. Instead I take Lucia outside twice, once in the morning to buy a piece of minute steak and then in the afternoon to walk around the block, pulling her on the sleigh. The snow walls reveal only the upper storeys of the houses. The sharply-cut drifts are layered like ancient stones: blue, pale grey, white, off-white. I run the last half block, pulling Lucia along, her laugh following me.

THE ART OF BURGLARY

I meet Lily and the twins waiting outside the door to my apartment. "We came down to find you two," Lily says. "Come up for a cuppa."

Lily's apartment floats in a sea of objects: clothes, toys, artificial flowers, ornaments, used dishes, records, boxes, catalogues, newspapers, ashtrays, cups and saucers. She sets the Brown Betty teapot down and takes out her Black Cat cigarettes. I hold Lucia on my lap, clearing a space on the table, putting objects out of reach of her questing hands.

"We got these great Joe Louis cakes at Steinberg's," Lily says. "Want to try one?" She holds out the plate. The twins, who had been lounging against the fridge, rush forward and grab the little cakes with both hands. "Give over, you monkeys." Lily laughs. She slaps at Nigel's hand, just as Rex swings his truck at her. I see a coloured blur as the truck misses his mother and connects with Lucia, slamming across her face.

Lucia screams, a long wrenching cry of terror and pain. I put my hand over the cut on her forehead, shuddering with fear. My guts twist as blood spurts through my fingers.

"I'll call a taxi to take you to emergency," Lily says.

The twins have disappeared. Lily brings a wet cloth to hold on the cut. "Oh dear God," I say, "Oh God help us." I go out without my coat, walking the hall by the front door, shushing the baby in my arms. We are both crying.

❖

133

When Paul comes home at suppertime, we lean over the crib, looking at our sleeping baby, a big Band-Aid over one eyebrow.

"The doctor said head cuts bleed a lot," I say, "The truck missed her eye, her temple. I didn't see it coming." I start to weep.

Paul puts an arm around my shoulder. "Listen Janet, why don't you stay away from that stupid woman upstairs and her gruesome brats? What's the attraction for you anyway? Just drop her."

"I owe her five dollars," I say. "For the taxi. Can you pay her?"

"I'll go up there tomorrow," he says, but, the next morning, he changes his mind. "It's going to cost us at least five to fix that gash in the wall. Tell her we'll use the five for that."

"But I never told her about it," I say, but he's out the door and gone. Lucia and I watch from the front window as his car heads into the snowflakes.

I met Captain Paul LaVoie at a party at a cottage in Muskoka. I was working then as an assistant librarian at the University of Toronto and a week later he showed up in full uniform to ask me out for supper at Fran's Restaurant. At the end of the wedding, in the chapel at Camp Borden, we emerged into a tunnel made of crossed swords held aloft by his fellow officers. I continued at the library for several months until he was posted to Valcartier, outside Quebec City. There were no jobs for an English-speaking librarian, but, by that time, I was pregnant anyway.

Shortly after we moved into the apartment on Rue Dollard des Ormeaux, he developed the habit

THE ART OF BURGLARY

of coming home late. There were always excuses: work, sports, a meeting, a special military exercise. At first, I thought he had found another woman, but Lily dropped many hints. Her man did not gamble. Her René did not spend every evening playing poker like some. Lucky for her, René came from a small village in the Gaspe and had no gang of friends in town to hang out with after work.

When I proffer a discussion, Paul throws up his hands, talks about trust. "Be serious, Janet. You know what job I have. I am in charge there and no one else. And I need your support." He tousles my hair as he leaves.

A faint, almost soundless knock. Lily stands in the hall, the twins behind her, no toys in hand. She holds out a small paper bag. "I brought some sweeties for the baby," she says. "How is she? Is she going to be all right?" She touches Lucia's cheek with one finger. "I'm so sorry Janet. Those brats of mine are so fast. René was furious. I couldn't sleep for worry."

At that minute, two young women, students at Laval who live on the third floor, come clattering down laughing and talking rapidly. Friends. They stand for a minute at the front door a half dozen steps up, buttoning their coats and putting on their gloves, the French words floating like unknown coins towards us. They turn and wave at us.

"Bonjour."

"Bonjour," we say.

As the outer door opens, the winter sun slashes across the marble floor, bounces off the brass mailboxes, swoops across the ceiling. One woman

135

holds the heavy door open for her friend and then also steps out into the winter brightness. I can hear the lilt of their voices even after the door swings shut.

I make up my mind.

"Come in, Lily," I say. "The baby is fine. I'll tell you all about it over a cup of tea."

CAN'T SEE A CLOUD IN THE SKY

Janet saw her first hippie in July, 1967, at Expo in Montreal. She and her husband, Paul, stood last in line to visit the Thai Pavilion. The sign beside them read, *Wait Time – One Hour.* The golden building was so extravagantly carved, gargoyled and ornamented, it glowed like the heart of the sun. But Janet knew where Paul's heart was—somewhere in the closest bar, nestled among the bottles of cold beer.

They had arrived at Expo 67 that morning having driven down the day before from the military base at Valcartier, where Paul, a captain in the Canadian army, was posted. That morning at Expo, they visited the American geodesic dome, the Man and His World photography exhibit, and the medieval art of the Belgium Pavilion. Paul sauntered through the buildings as Janet related all the interesting facts from her guidebook. She longed to see everything: the films at the Czech Pavilion, the Russian dancers, the Jamaican bands.

For lunch, they picked the Japanese restaurant because it had the shortest line-up. Inside, Paul glowered down at the table set with unfamiliar lacquer dishes, carved chopsticks and an iron teapot on an ornate stand. For a minute, she thought he would stand up and leave. Instead, he picked up the chopsticks between a finger and thumb and waved them at the traditionally coifed and robed hostess. "A knife and fork, if you please," he said. His voice rattled the white paper screen beside them.

When his teriyaki came, he ate half-heartedly, stirring the items around his plate looking for bits of beef, finding a piece, stabbing it, lifting it part way to his mouth to stare at it for a minute, as if he expected it would bite back. The hostess, smelling of spices and jasmine, stood behind Janet's chair. She put her hand over Janet's to show her how to use the chopsticks to lift the little rice cakes called sushi. She giggled when Janet dropped them on the plate and clapped happily when she succeeded in getting one to her mouth, but she also handed her a fork and smiled.

With a graceful side-swoop of her long sleeve, the hostess' delicate hand lifted the teapot to pour the pale steaming liquid into two tiny china cups. Paul merely stared at his and slugged back on his bottle of Japanese beer. When the hostess moved on to the next table, Janet read aloud the information in the guidebook about the Thai exhibit, trying to awaken a modicum of enthusiasm in her husband.

Now standing in the heat in the Thai line-up, she knew Paul's patience was dragging to an end. Every attraction within view had long tails of waiting people and the sidewalks were becoming more crowded every minute. Above them, everything soared: the parabolas and swooping curves of the Russian and Canadian Pavilions and the elegant loops of the monorail overhead, calligraphy against the sky. All the national flags danced on tall poles. A marching band came by with acrobats. Women in cotton dresses and men in short-sleeved summer shirts drifted happily along eating ice cream and hot dogs. The noise of the train, the hum and murmur of the crowd, the smells, a mixture of spices and mustard and hot pavements, energized her. On the far end of the island, the American dome, a gigantic toy ball, seemed ready to sail into the blue sky. She was in fairyland. She wanted to walk in every direction at once, see it all.

"Oh, look over there, Paul." Janet pointed to the narrow canal that ran beside the pavilion. The royal barge of Thailand, half hidden by the green bank, floated in carved splendour, the curve of the prow swooping up to a golden dragon head sparking with glass jewels. She opened her guidebook to find the description.

"Look at that guy," her husband interrupted. "What a get-up. They should toss the bum out."

A man in a strange garb was walking directly towards them, smiling. His thick brown hair hung in waves almost to his shoulders. Strangely, he wore shorts, practical in the hot July weather but wildly inappropriate here. Janet had never seen a grown man in shorts before, except in photos of Australian soldiers. He had a beard, a full brown bush on his lower face. He looked like Charles Dickens or Charles Darwin or perhaps Karl Marx, a creature dropped from the 19th century. His muscular hairy legs ended in large dusty feet encased in sandals of the sort seen in Biblical illustrations. Over one shoulder, he carried a canvas knapsack like those used by fishermen. It was difficult to look at him without smiling, and she realized he was beaming back at her as he approached. Was he actually going to speak to them?

"What the hell does he want?" Paul muttered. "Hang on to your purse." He moved closer to stand behind her.

"Hi," the strange person said in a deep voice. "You guys look so hot and bothered at the end of the line, I thought I'd come over and give you a tip." He lowered his voice. "If you want to get into this pavilion, do what I did—sneak in the back way. Just slip around the corner and you'll find a little door. Once you're inside, mingle about. Far out place, Thailand. Wild art. Good vibes."

They stared, speechless.

"This has been the best week of my life," he went on. "I'm having a ball. I've been here every day. All you need is a jar of yogurt, some sandwiches and hard-boiled eggs and just take it as it comes, go with the flow, you know what I'm saying?" Beside her, she heard Paul grunt. The young man hitched up his knapsack. "Take it easy now," he waved as he strode off, his sandals flapping along the path.

"That was a hippie," Janet said. "I'm sure of it." She'd read about hippies in *Life* magazine. The article said they lived together in great clumps in San Francisco and, for an unknown reason, never cut their hair or washed.

Her husband was muttering again. "Do you really want to see this Thailand place, Janet? Let's get out of here before any more weirdoes bother us."

"How about sneaking in the back door," she said hopefully.

He looked at her, appalled. In an hour, her husband's long-time friend, Jean-Guy Pelletier, who lived in Montreal, was arriving at the Expo train station. "Why don't we just stroll along, see if we can get on the monorail," Janet suggested.

"Too many people," he said. "With President De Gaulle traipsing around, half the pavilions are closed. And that's another bum they should have thrown out."

Her husband was a fervent anti-Separatist, still angry about De Gaulle's performance the night before. On the hotel TV, they'd watched amazed as the French president, on the balcony of Montreal City Hall, called out, "Vive Le Québec libre! Vive le Québec libre!" his arms outstretched like Christ offering salvation to the ecstatic crowd. The Canadian officials beside him stood frozen in place.

Their friend Jean-Guy was a half-hearted Separatist, or at least he was last year when he visited their home on the Valcartier army base. If Jean-Guy's views had hardened since then, she worried, the two men might quarrel. But it seemed impossible, such good friends from childhood. Nevertheless, the topic was incendiary. Last week, at a house party on the base, a shouting match erupted. The hostess rushed to calm the two men but retreated in tears. Janet felt the atmosphere change as a rush of insecurity and violence swept through the room only to dissipate a few seconds later after one of the shouters stormed out.

Now, to calm her thoughts, Janet visualized the hippie. She recalled a detail. "What's yogurt, anyway?" she said to Paul.

"How should I know?" he replied.

Jean-Guy was waiting inside the turnstile. "Bon jour, bon jour, mon capitaine," he cried, making fun of Paul's army rank. He air-kissed Janet smackingly on both cheeks. "Ma Belle Janet," he said. "Lovely to see you again."

The conversation switched to French. "No dinner at the French Pavilion, mon ami," Paul said. "De Gaulle is dining there."

"No problem. We'll find something."

"I didn't want to go to the French Pavilion anyway," Janet said and she read in English from a clipping she had put into her guidebook. "Displayed on the roof of the French Pavilion, the papier-mâché figures impaled atop the art machines symbolize the passive female; the motor-driven clanking robots represent the active male."

The two men stopped and looked at her, their faces carefully composed. They did not smirk, but she had a feeling they would later, when she could not see them.

Jean-Guy took her hand. "Ah Janet. Some silly French intellectual wrote that. Quel idiot. Come on now. I've known you for years and you never seemed the passive type to me. Non, non. C'est vrai, n'est pas, Paul?"

142

THE ART OF BURGLARY

Her husband smiled and hugged her hard around the waist. "Pas ma femme. One cool chick. She forced me to take this trip. Before I knew what was happening, she had the whole thing arranged and I was driving down the highway."

As they continued walking, Janet tried to figure it all out. She was not sure if she was the passive type or not. But what did it matter, really? She was just a solitaire inside a group labeled passive, a label stuck on to her and on all her friends so that, in a small way, it coloured their world. She knew some women made use of the label, acted dumb and passive, waved their arms like children and said, I couldn't possibly do this or that. But that wasn't her nature. Her friends sometimes remarked what a fearless driver she was. "I could never go to the Lower Town with all those narrow streets," one said, and suddenly, she saw them all as cowards, all these women who took advantage.

They were headed for the twin pavilions of Man the Producer and Man the Provider. It was midafternoon and the crowds seemed thicker than ever, a slow river of people who were quieter somehow, but perhaps that was her imagination. The three could no longer walk side by side. It had become so hot that it was surprising to see so many men in jackets, some in heavy cotton windbreakers and others in long denim jackets zipped up close.

Ahead of her, Paul and Jean-Guy moved close together, their voices drifting back to her in a waterfall of almost incomprehensible French slang and private jokes punctuated by the occasional laugh. At first, she was able to stay close behind them. The odd word or phrase came to her: Pearson, pure laine, De Gaulle, les ans noirs, John Flag, their nickname for Montreal mayor Jean Drapeau. They were nattering on about separatism, but, at least, they weren't arguing.

But the two men were walking too quickly, threading their way easily, as if they were one person. Several other people filled the space in front of her, so that now she could barely see them. A Mountie in full uniform pushed past her and, a few steps later, pushed past her husband. Paul took a step backward and suddenly there was something else. Jean Guy put his fingers on his lips and then slowly ran them across Paul's cheek or at least she thought that was what happened. Her husband's face had been turned away from her and she only saw it when he looked at his companion and smiled. The gesture, if it happened at all, seemed too strange, almost like blowing a kiss.

Janet stopped and let the crowd jostle around her. The monorail, a great swooping sky cat, screamed overhead; a group of Newfoundland clog dancers clattered together on a low platform off to one side; the calls from an ice cream vendor rose past the fiddle music. His jokes in slangy French had the crowd laughing.

She no longer could see them. At lunch they'd agreed if one got lost they'd go to the bar in the Ontario Pavilion and wait for the other. She consulted her map, walking and thinking.

It seemed odd she allowed herself to get distracted so easily. Was it an unconscious move to get a moment of freedom, to walk alone and let her happiness take over, to feel more expansive, her body looser? At the same time she found herself searching for the hippie, to see him striding along, for she imagined he would stride, looking around and taking everything in, breathing in the entire kaleidoscope and enjoying it all just as she was, now that she could set her own pace.

Something about the hippie fascinated her. Not the strange garb, his dusty feet in sandals, the startling beard. He was not a handsome man, not the least bit attractive to her as a man. Then what? She decided it was his expression. It was filled with a simple delight, an enjoyment of the world, a readiness to see and enjoy more. She'd never encountered that before. If she saw him, would she cry out, "See, I'm going with the flow," and laugh? Or would she? She wasn't sure.

So, now the Ontario Pavilion appeared. Once inside, she turned into the dimness of the bar, and made for a barstool. She was surprised to see how few customers had discovered this cool and shadowy oasis away from the heat and noise outside. She smoothed the skirt of her blue cotton dress and climbed up, relieved to set down her purse which held her heavy guidebook. The leather of the purse was warm, as if it had been cooking on a heater. It felt good to drop it at her feet. Along with the guidebook, it held only a lipstick, a comb and a few dollars, but she had felt it becoming heavier, felt the narrow strap cutting into her shoulder at the neck.

"Excuse me." A man in a dark suit with the Ontario trillium logo on the pocket was standing behind her swinging chair. "Are you waiting for someone?"

"Yes," she said. The bartender stood facing her on the far side of the counter, his eyes on the logo man, his head on one side, waiting.

"Who're you waiting for?"

"My husband." As she said the words, she wondered why she was asked and moreover, why she had automatically replied.

The man turned and walked away and she swung around to give her order to the bartender, but he'd disappeared to the other side of the circular bar. Through the stacks of bottles and glasses she could see him talking to a young couple.

Now another man was behind her, the same jacket, same logo. "You're waiting for your husband. How long will he be?"

"I don't know." She smiled. Why had she answered so unthinkingly? Why had she smiled?

"You don't know?"

She felt herself getting annoyed. "No, I do not."

He left, following the route of the first man to the hall. Two burly men in zipped-up denim jackets arrived, their round bullet heads dripping with sweat. They took seats at the far end of the bar. The bartender brought them each a beer and one held the bottle up to his heat-reddened face.

Both Ontario Pavilion guys were back. "We think you'd be more comfortable if you waited for your husband at one of the tables."

THE ART OF BURGLARY

"I'm fine here."

"You won't be served here. But you will be at a table." He made a little head waiter bow, as if in an expensive restaurant.

She got up, retrieved her purse and walked to the nearest table. Her face burned, but no one in the bar seemed to notice. It was a large room. Sound was swallowed up. The logo men had been talking so quietly she was sure no one overheard. But why could she not sit at the bar like a normal person? Last night at the hotel, she and Paul had sat at the bar where they had watched the De Gaulle fiasco on the hotel bar's TV. She had the feeling that she might cry. She was not sure why.

The bartender took her order and, at last, an icy rye and ginger ale was placed in front of her. She could not look up at him. She kept her head down searching for something in her purse. She knew her cheeks were flaming.

Ten minutes later Paul and Jean-Guy walked in. They called out for beer and Paul said to the bartender, "Turn up the TV. Pearson is speaking." Like the man in the denim jacket at the end of the bar, Paul held the bottle to his cheek.

She told them what happened to her.

"He thought you were a prostitute," Jean-Guy said.

"What!" She looked at Paul for help, but the TV blared forth and they just caught Prime Minister Pearson's words before his round baby face disappeared from the screen. Janet could barely focus. She knew her face was red with anger and with something else, the shame of the insult, the terrible, incomprehensible knowledge that it happened at all.

"Merde!" Jean-Guy said. "That was short and to the point. Basically Pearson told him, shut your face, Monsieur De Gaulle."

The bartender came over with two more beer. He did not look at her. She downed the rye. She felt reckless, the insult burning. She stood up to face him. "So," she said, her face all frown. She was going to say, "Do you still think I'm a prostitute," but then realized he could still think it but now with clients.

"Leave it alone, Janet," her husband said, standing up and taking her by the arm. But he froze at the words of the news announcer. "The French President is leaving Canada." Everyone in the bar turned.

"President Charles De Gaulle, upon hearing Prime Minister Pearson's speech, has decided he will leave Expo at once, where he has been touring the various pavilions. CBC has also learned that the French president will depart by special jet tomorrow afternoon and return to France, cancelling his official trip to Ottawa."

The two men looked at each other. "If he's at the French Pavilion, his car has to come along the main road out there," Jean-Guy said. "Let's get outside. I want to cheer him on."

"You idiot," Paul said glaring at his friend. The two did not speak as they walked to the door with Janet after them. She felt glad to leave the hateful place. Her legs felt weak with anger. Her husband had not stood up for her. Not one bit. 'Leave it

THE ART OF BURGLARY

Janet.' The words burned as if nothing out of the ordinary had happened.

Outside, between the buildings and along the roadway, a great crowd was massing. The sound of the voices swelled but softly, as if the people were connected to each other by a giant whisper. Silently, the three of them stood for what seemed to her a long time. Pencil lines of sunlight angled down, touching the patient faces, the mopping handkerchiefs. The faint sounds of a marching band came at them from the next building, although which country it represented she could not remember. Just after the music jarred to a stop she found herself face-to-face with a man in a denim jacket.

"If you call out or boo or cheer when De Gaulle's limousine comes by, you will be arrested," he said, his voice firm. His head, which seemed to waver in the heat, leaned forward towards them and then to the people on either side. Repeating the same words in French, he stopped before two teen-agers nearby and then an elderly couple who goggled at him, their mouths open. He wheeled around to push farther back into the crowd. Janet could see more men, other jackets, walking towards the rear when everyone else was straining forward towards the road, and she saw they were threading back and forth, their lips barely moving, but she was sure the same warning was repeated.

"Plain clothes," her husband whispered. "La Sûreté."

A wave of anger struck her as if the pressure of a giant will, the sort found in totalitarian countries, had been clamped upon her.

"This is terrible," she said out loud. "How dare they silence us! I hope someone cheers."

"Don't say a word, Janet," her husband said. "Toi aussi," he said to Jean-Guy. "I won't bail you out. You'll have to beg a long time."

Jean-Guy's face was purple with rage. "Calice! I don't believe this." He turned away. "I'm going home."

Paul looked stunned. His hand reached out to his friend's shoulder.

"I can't stay for this shit," Jean-Guy said and then something else in French, quite low, that sounded like "deux semaines."

For a minute, her husband stared after his departing friend, but then he slowly turned in a circle, his attention fixed on the crowd, scanning it carefully. Taller than most people, he was watching the plain clothes police at work, his slight smirk denoting something. She realized it was admiration for how they did their job, swiftly, coldly, as out of place as sharks in a fish tank but sharks just the same.

A jostling happened. Janet found herself propelled forward through a gap, past a woman's bare arm. She was now close to the road. Through the heat, a series of black vehicles advanced slowly toward them. She was struck by the absurdity of the situation, the nuttiness of being told that she would be arrested if she made a sound.

"I hope someone boos," she said.

Her husband had moved up behind her. "Shhh," he said.

She longed for her fellow countrymen to disobey, to boo, or shout "Vive le Québec libre," and, if everyone did it, she thought, they could not all be arrested. One person just had to start and she too would join in even if it were vive le Québec libre, those terrible, provocative words. Yes, even those words. Yes, she'd join in to show she was a free person in a free country.

The first cars passed slowly and then the long black limo, its windows shadowy. Inside, barely visible, sat a tall man looking straight ahead. But not one voice, not even a partial voice, not one sound, as if even whispers had been forbidden and so, she too, stood mute, like all the others. She felt ashamed in some confusing way that this had happened at all. Almost immediately, people began to move, disperse out to the road. The marching band in the next building started up again.

They walked in silence to the train station, Paul with his usual sauntering walk. He was not the least bit tired and she saw he was glancing around now and then, on the lookout for Jean-Guy. She took his arm. He had not seemed too upset by Jean-Guy's exit. The old friendship remained. But she herself felt dreadfully worn-out, her body aching in every muscle. Also, she was afraid that they would get separated again.

Only two weeks ago she'd begged Paul to take her to Expo, and, after a few days he had relented, even though he had not the slightest interest in art or displays from far-off countries. She believed he only agreed to please her. At the time, she felt grateful.

But now she thought she should have come alone, even if every one of their friends and relatives remarked on it. But how much better if she had come by herself! None of this would have happened. She realized she was confused about what this was exactly. What did Jean-Guy mean, 'deux semaines?' She'd not asked and the moment passed. She'd ask later, but how strange that she felt reluctant, as if a genuine answer would not be forthcoming. Her mind turned again to the episode in the bar, her automatic acquiescence to the horrible logo men. That's what made her so angry. Not Jean-Guy's remark so much as her own passivity, as passive as the papier-mâché sculptures on the roof of the French Pavilion. She rubbed her forehead. She must stop obsessing about the scene in the bar. It was eating her up.

They'd go to their hotel, have a good dinner and drive back to Base Valcartier in the morning to resume their lives as army officer and army officer's wife. On the crowded train platform, they stood together in line, the colourful banners snapping above them in the dry hot wind. The recorded music changed. "I Only Have Eyes for You," sang Mario Lanza's sharp tenor voice. Paul was checking the tickets and humming along. The slick blue train slid soundlessly into the station.

"Can't see a cloud in the sky," her husband mouthed with the music, his hand on her arm as he guided her into the train.

THE YEGG BOY

"The Yegg Boy is in the paper," her husband says at the door of the greenhouse.

"What?" Janet has not heard the name for thirty years.

He steps just inside the doorframe, holding the newspaper to shelter it from the sharp May wind. "It seems they're digging up the old graves at First Presbyterian to make room for the expansion, and," he reads, "among the early residents whose remains are to be removed tomorrow, only one achieved fame or rather notoriety—eight-year-old Thomas Randall Teasdale, known as the Yegg Boy, whose death at Victoria School in 1908 is still a mystery."

Janet waits a moment and then says, "So, his middle name was Randall. I didn't know that."

Janet first learns about the Yegg Boy in August, 1982, the day she arrives at the small town of Port Gill to check a hundred-year-old elementary school building and report on its suitability for heritage status. She's divorced, in her mid-forties, and a researcher with Ontario Heritage. She sings as she drives, glad to be out of the Toronto heat, out of the archives, and out in the field, a simple task ahead, one she knows she'll enjoy. A piece of cake day.

The morning mist from Lake Ontario shimmers across Highway 401 as she takes the exit, dropping down towards the lake, moving past a couple of gas stations and fast food joints to enter, unexpectedly, a street of mature trees, great oaks and maples, whose branches half-hide an exuberance of Victoriana: brick, stone and half-timbered houses, many flaunting towers or turrets, wrap-around porches or glassed-in verandas.

What good luck to come across such an old-fashioned parade, she thinks as she checks the street sign on the corner. Empire Street. Could any name be more fitting? She'll walk back later and take notes. She knows, of course, that Port Gill holds many more modest streets, but she loves the wealthy imprint of a vanished age so often found in small Southern Ontario towns, especially those that front on Lake Ontario or Lake Erie.

How different from the northern town where she grew up with its haphazard shapelessness. As usual, the thought of Port Arthur triggers an inward wince, the remnant of a time where every face knew her story and where, it seemed, she could not turn a corner without running into her ex-husband, usually with *her* on his arm. She flings aside the flick of humiliation and resolutely turns the Honda into Port Gill's main drag: a boxy line of shops, a few shuttered and closed, and two stately bank buildings, also worth a look later.

THE ART OF BURGLARY

Ahead, the old school almost has her slamming on the brakes. She pulls over to take it in. The building stretches across the top of the street, golden pink and solid, two storeys of Port Credit sandstone set in a half circle of green lawn. On the second floor, above the double oak doors, she sees the famous round window, the jewel that will save the building from the wrecking ball. The window is the focus of the street. At least ten feet in diameter, made of radiating coloured glass panels, it resembles a multi-coloured daisy, its circular centre containing a painted glass portrait, the head and shoulders of old Queen Victoria herself, presenting her pudgy profile to the street below.

The building breathes the 1880s, and Sir Wilfrid Laurier and the twentieth century belonging to Canada. Janet does not have to see the opening day photograph to envision the top hats, the substantial stomachs, the gold watch chains, and the respectful crowd in the background, and later, when she sees the actual picture, she's not far wrong.

"Would you like to see the place where they found the murdered child?" the school principal, Mark Ryko, asks.

The outlandish question snaps her back. They're standing in the wide front hall of the school, looking at portraits of former principals and she's been musing how pleasantly inefficient the old architects were with entrance space. The hall and two sweeping staircases take up almost the entire ground floor. The downstairs contains only three classrooms, all lined up across the back.

"A murdered child? Oh my God! How awful!"

Mark Ryko smiles at her. "No, no. Don't be upset. It was a long time ago, 1908 to be exact. Let me show you."

She's spent the morning with Ryko and, so far, she likes him. She admires his easy rapport with the teachers they met as they toured the classrooms. He's a stocky man, with a wide smile and a purposeful walk, shorter than she and perhaps a year or two younger. Now, she follows him under one of the staircases—marked girls' stairs on the original plans—through a small door, down a flight of oak steps scooped out by the passing of countless little feet and into a low-ceilinged basement room.

Mark explains. "For many years, this basement was divided into two sections, a girls' basement and a boys'. This was the girls' side. Far as I know, no amenities. The kids just ran around, I guess. And during the baby boom years, they actually set up classrooms down here. Then for a while it was a playroom. Now, of course, we have the gymnasium in the new wing."

Janet shudders inwardly at the mention of the new wing, an aluminum extrusion mercifully hidden at the back of the building. Still, she thinks even a 1960's utility box is preferable to this dungeon space with its deep-set, barred windows.

The principal points to a roughened patch on the concrete floor. "Here's where they found the

THE ART OF BURGLARY

body, face down in a pool of cement. Found on a Monday morning in April 1908. On the Friday before, a crew of workmen dug the pit and filled it in with cement. Then on Monday, when they arrived, they found the child. At first they thought he'd fallen down the stairs, landed in the wet slurry and drowned. Now, here's the mystery. He hadn't drowned. He'd been hanged or maybe strangled, no one knows for sure."

"Strangled. Hanged? Oh, the poor child!" Janet feels a shiver of horror as she stares at the rough patch easily visible on the scuffed floor. "How does a school pupil get hanged?"

"There was an inquest, of course," Mark says. "The clippings are upstairs, if you're interested."

"A boy. How old?"

"Eight," Mark says, "And supposedly small for his age. Very little known about him except his name was Thomas Teasdale."

"Thomas Teasdale," she says slowly. "Such a melodious name. His parents must have been devastated."

"Ah, well, he wasn't called Thomas you see. Everyone—except the teachers, I hope—called him the Yegg Boy."

She'd come across the word before. An old Canadian word. A yegg was a sort of tramp—or thief. A general no-good. "Whoa," she says, incredulous. "They called an eight-year-old boy a yegg?"

"Rough times, then. The child had no parents. He was more or less a homeless kid. Apparently, he sometimes stayed with an uncle, a bad character, but that guy was in the Don Jail the day the kid was murdered. No one was ever charged. I often wonder how hard the cops worked to find the killer of a kid from Tarpaper Town."

"Tarpaper Town?" she says. "That's not on the old maps."

"Oh, they never are," Mark says as he leads the way up to the second floor and toward the front of the building. He holds open the door of the teachers' room and the coloured window leaps into view, sending red, yellow and green lights wheeling around the walls. Up close, Queen Victoria looks even more disgruntled than she did from the street. Quickly, Mark pulls the cords that allow long drapes to settle across the window, muting the flying colours. "Drives you crazy, sometimes," he says, "as if you've fallen into a pit of fireworks or an explosion in a paint factory. No one knows who designed it. The town loves it, of course." He rummages in a filing cabinet and brings out a folder of Xeroxed newspaper clippings.

"Coffee?" he asks.

Janet nods and, while he fills the pot at the counter, she takes her high-powered magnifying glass from her purse and applies it to the cramped 1908 newspaper lettering, her pity for the child deepening as she reads.

According to the coroner, a Dr. Sewell, "the Teasdale boy died of strangulation at least two days before the body was discovered. Two marks circled the child's neck, a higher line close to the ears, consistent with a hanging and another circular mark lower down where the kerchief around his

THE ART OF BURGLARY

neck had been tightened." Once again Janet feels a shudder. "Massive damage to the windpipe," the doctor testified, "but I cannot say with certainty which injury was the chief cause of death."

"So, someone hanged him and then changed their mind and strangled him?" Janet says to Mark trying for a light tone to counteract the horror she feels.

"Seems insane, doesn't it?" He puts two mugs of coffee on the table, adding a bowl of sugar and a small carton of cream from the miniature fridge.

Janet reads on. The principal at the time, a Mr. Greenwood, also testified. According to him, little Thomas had made a rare appearance at school. Besides being a poor attender, he was a poor student as well. "It seems," she says to Mark, "that the child had the bad taste to faint during morning assembly and fall part way down the main staircase." She says this making a query face.

"They stood on the stairs, Janet, for the assembly—the boys on the boys' stairs and the girls on their side."

"They stood?"

"Well, they didn't have folding chairs in those days, I imagine. Yes, they stood every Friday morning as long as an hour or even more. Mostly hymns, prayers, patriotic songs and so on. Some of the old programs are in the board archives."

Janet goes back to the clippings. Little Thomas was taken to the lady teachers' room and was allowed to lie down for half an hour. Then, as punishment—for fainting?—the principal decreed the child be kept in at recess. However, at the end of the morning, he seemed so sickly, his teacher, a Miss Evelyn Carstairs, sent him home.

"How do you send a homeless child home?" Janet asks.

Mark shakes his head, raises his coffee mug.

The jury came to the school to examine the cement pit where the body was found. The school was installing sewers for the first time and a set of toilets in each basement area. The pit was the place where the inside and outside pipes connected. The area was about five feet square and, on this Friday, the workmen had mixed the cement, filled in the hole, smoothed it over, taken their tools and left, leaving their foreman, Salvatore Maltese, to lock both the inside and outside basement doors and take the keys to the principal. The keys were kept on a hook in the principal's office.

The principal, who seemed to be the major testifier at the inquest, said: "I went into the basement a few minutes after the crew left. I checked the cement work"—no small body lying there presumably—"checked the new sanitary facilities and then returned to my office on the second floor after I relocked the basement. Forty minutes later, the vice principal and I left the building. We were the last ones to leave. As was our custom, we walked around the building to make sure all the outer doors were completely secure."

The last to testify was Thomas' teacher, Miss Evelyn Carstairs. She simply corroborated what the principal said and added, "the child seemed so pale and faint by lunch time that I sent him home."

THE ART OF BURGLARY

Did he have breakfast that day? Janet wonders. *Did no one think to feed the poor creature? Apparently not.* She stares at the only illustration on the page, a line drawing depicting Miss Carstairs' very young and pretty face under a sweep of hat and upswept hair. Obviously, she alone caught the artist's eye. No picture of Thomas Teasdale, unfortunately.

Janet puts down her coffee cup and unrolls her blueprints and building plans. The original building had no bathrooms—not even in the two teachers' rooms, the men's in which they are now sitting and the lady teachers' room, a windowless box, also on the second floor.

She finds the 1908 blueprint for the *new* basement washrooms, two toilets in each section of the basement, unpartitioned from each other and beside them a separate cubicle marked *teacher*. It must have seemed to everyone, teachers and pupils alike, that progress was evolving as it should, especially when they recalled the long icy trip across the playground to the outhouse in winter.

"It really is very simple," Janet says, picking up the cup which Mark had refilled. "The teacher dismissed the boy. Instead of going home, he hid himself somewhere inside the school and then, when everyone was gone, and the school was empty—"

"Murdered himself and threw himself into the pit," Mark interrupts with a rueful smile. "Somehow getting through a locked door on the way."

"OK," Janet smiles. "It must have been the principal. He alone had the key."

161

"And the motive?" Mark says. "Fainting during Friday assembly? Rough discipline even for those days." He puts down his coffee cup. "Actually, the foreman, Maltese, was the suspect, of course, a foreigner and all. And on top of that, he left town after the murder and was never seen again. Probably a wise move." He stands up. "There are another couple of articles in the last folder if you want to read on." He rinses his cup at the little sink and sets it on the drain. "Unfortunately, I have to get back to work here. Three hundred little screamers arriving next week. I want to be ready. If possible."

"Will any of them be poor and homeless?"

"Ah indeed." His sigh turns into a sort of hopeless groan, and he says, "No doubt, no doubt." As he moves toward the door, he says, "I'll be in my office if you need anything."

Janet stares into space, her imagination netted by the story of the Yegg Boy. The school settles into a half silence. She hears the janitor's floor polisher from the first floor and the scrape of a file drawer from Mark's office next door. It's eleven o'clock. Even with the curtains closed, colours vibrate across the walls and across the papers spread on the table.

She regards Queen Victoria, barely seen through the drapes, portly and relaxed, in the hub of her coloured wheel. Did little Thomas Teasdale ever stand in front of this beautiful window? Probably not, although he may have stood in the principal's office next door and been bawled out for fainting, or missing school, or for generally having committed the sin of being poor and malnourished and ill.

Janet leans over the two remaining clippings on the table. A little more information about Thomas. He had no address. Sometimes he slept in the back shed of a *confectionery* in Tarpaper Town. The last clipping was an editorial from the Port Gill *News Leader*. It suggested rounding up all homeless boys and putting them in an orphanage where they'd get a good Christian training. It also suggested burning down Tarpaper Town. "Do we need slums," the editor said, "which encourage all sorts of disgusting habits and harbour degraded foreigners? Tarpaper Town should be wiped off the face of the earth."

No wonder Maltese had skipped.

Mark is not in his office when she looks in; perhaps he already went for lunch, so after a quick hamburger from a restaurant on the main street, she retrieves her collection of picks and scrapers from the Honda, intending to take a preliminary look at the original paint colours. She starts in the primary room on the first floor, a big classroom with high windows, a long separate cloakroom and a walk-in supply closet. Pushing aside a tall bookcase at the back, she slices away a sliver of paint, expecting to come across layer upon layer of colour. Instead, a few slices down, she arrives at a black stain, obviously charcoal, the evidence of a fire.

At that moment, Violet Smith, the primary teacher, who Janet met earlier that morning, walks in carrying an armload of books. She reminds Janet of Queen Victoria in the window, the same soft face and severe grey hair, but, quite possibly, unlike Queen Victoria, Miss Violet Smith's voice reveals the careful enunciation of the long-time primary teacher.

"Oh, Miss Smith," Janet calls out. "Did you ever have a fire here?"

Violet Smith immediately halts, her pudgy face whitening as the stack of books in her arms cascade and clatter across the floor. Her hands fly to her mouth and she moans as if in pain.

Janet stares at the teacher in astonishment. "I'm so sorry. I didn't mean to upset you," she says.

Surprisingly Violet Smith throws back her head and laughs loudly. "I suppose they're not going to dismiss me a year before my retirement. They do say, sins will out, and so they do, indeed."

"Sins?"

"It was a pathetic sin, really," Violet Smith says. "You see, there used to be a door at the back of this classroom, close to where you're standing. It led directly out to the playground. And here," she gestured, "just inside, the teachers on yard duty sheltered on cold days. We had a small spirit lamp in the supply cupboard, safely hidden behind some books. We boiled water and made tea and watched the children through the big windows."

Janet is not sure she understands. "And this was the sin?"

"Oh, glory! It was so cold sometimes. And we were out half an hour at a time, from eight-thirty to nine in the morning and often the entire lunch hour. We were never allowed a break in those days.

THE ART OF BURGLARY

Recess was just another work time. So, my dear, every day, a secret tea party in this room."

She gathers the books from the floor before continuing. "When I started teaching, I inherited the tea set." She smiles proudly. "I was told the secret tea parties had been going on ever since the school opened in 1883. Of course, you can understand, I was terribly nervous about being caught. We all were. Terrified. But I did love my cup of tea."

"Terrified?" Janet says. It seems a strange word to use in the circumstances.

"Oh yes. You see, the principal and the vice-principal were always upstairs in the men teachers' room." Violet Smith chuckles softly as she places the books on a small desk. "We often said what a mercy it was that the men teachers' room overlooked the main street and not the playground."

"And you were never discovered?"

"No, never. But, oh my, that fire was a close call. It was in 1935, my first year. A book or some papers, I've never been sure exactly, just burst into flames and the fire shot right up that wall with a flash!" Violet Smith covers her eyes with her hands as if blocking out the sight. Her entire body gives a little tremor as she continues. "A second later, Evelyn had it doused with our water jug. The room filled up with black smoke. Simply terrifying. Someone opened the outside door, I don't remember who. I was in hysterics. Terrible, terrible." She shakes her head as if to clear it. "Such a close call."

Janet tries to unravel the story. "I'm not sure I understand, Violet. Why were you so upset, if the fire was quickly put out and there was no damage to speak of?"

Violet Smith looks at Janet as if she were a pupil who'd given a particularly foolish answer. "That was a different time, Miss Marsden. The Great Depression. And no union then, my dear! Quite simply, we all—all four of us—would have been fired. We did stop meeting for tea for a while, but I'm afraid we drifted back. Anyway, it wasn't long after, some time during the war I think, the whole arrangement came to an end. Yard duty was reduced and we were sent out only two at a time and the men had to take their share as well. Hallelujah! We could go up to the lady teachers' room. We took the tea things up there and bought a little hot plate..."

Janet isn't listening; she's staring. One word lingers in her mind. "Evelyn? Did you say Evelyn?"

"Yes, Evelyn Carstairs. She had the room next door. She was always so calm and quick. The next day, she brought some paint and at noon hour..."

Was it possible? How could the Evelyn Carstairs of the 1908 newspaper drawing, the upswept hat and high lace collar—how could that Miss Carstairs have anything to do with the fire in 1935?

"It can't be the same one," Janet blurts. "Thomas Teasdale's teacher?"

Violet Smith's smile disappears. "Evelyn Carstairs taught here for forty-eight years. We became very good friends. She helped me so much.

THE ART OF BURGLARY

It was very difficult in those days, you have no idea."

"What did she say about Thomas?"

"Oh, my! A dreadful experience for her. She said it was the most terrifying thing that ever happened to her, but having survived that, she felt she could survive anything."

"Survived it?" Again, a strange turn of phrase. "What did she mean?"

"Why, she was sure she'd be fired, of course," Violet Smith says. "In those days, you lost your job over the slightest breach of the rules and her principal then was a tyrant, she often told me that. Of course, principals were expected to be tyrants. Things are a good deal better..."

"But what rule had she broken?"

"Sending a child home at lunch hour without permission. Goodness, one didn't do anything without permission. She couldn't sleep for weeks thinking that any minute she'd be called into the office. She told me she used to shake with fright every time the principal looked at her."

Now it's Janet's turn to shake her head. "It seems crazy to me. A child faints in the morning. Had he eaten breakfast? Did anyone ask? He's allowed to lie down for a while and then punished by being kept back at recess and finally sent home. Sent home to where? And after he's found dead, his teacher can only think of her breach of the rules?"

Violet Smith's jowly face reddens. "Well, Evelyn didn't know this child. Classes were huge in those days, forty or more sometimes, and that boy hardly ever attended. Besides there was that other thing.

He was one of those children who smelled. We hardly get children like that nowadays. They were quite common once upon a time. Evelyn made him spend the entire morning in the cloakroom and she told me she considered leaving him there for the rest of the day. I know that sounds terrible, but, my dear, those were different times, crueler times, I'm afraid. And the child was from Tarpaper Town. I remember everyone was so glad when they finally burned it down..."

"But what did Miss Carstairs think happened to Thomas?"

"Oh, she believed he wandered back into the building in the afternoon and hid himself away and then, when everyone went home, he went down into the girl's basement and fell into that cement pit. He probably fainted again."

"But he was murdered."

Violet Smith looks momentarily startled. "Well, that's what some say," she says. "Even now people still say that. Even now." She turns and heads out the classroom door. "I have to get more supplies," she says and is gone.

Evelyn Carstairs is right. Her 1908 principal was a tyrant. Janet spends the next morning at the Board of Education office running through all the old files. In the twelve years of Mr. Greenwood's reign, there were over a dozen requests to the trustees to fire a teacher, most on the grounds of *improper conduct*. Several were indeed fired as the minutes showed, one young woman for attending the Roman Catholic Church with a friend and another accused of becoming inebriated at a house party. In 1899, a young male teacher was fired for leaving his classroom at lunchtime while a student was standing in the corner as punishment. A ruthless man, the principal. Yet his personnel report was exemplary. The trustees approved of his methods. "He is fair and firm with both staff and students," was a typical comment found in the minutes of 1908.

The 1907 minutes spoke of hiring a lady teacher, Miss Evelyn Carstairs, sixteen years of age, and a new male teacher as well—his salary to be $600.00 per annum and hers $325.00—and listed the staff for the coming year, four lady teachers for the primary grades and three men, including Mr. Greenwood, for the seniors.

Janet makes a few quick calculations. The sixteen-year-old Evelyn Carstairs was to teach for 48 more years and retire in 1956, close to half a century in the same school, outliving by a long way tyrannical principals. If Violet Smith started teaching in 1935, she spent twenty-one years in the classroom next to that of Evelyn Carstairs. The solid linkage of present and past is astonishing and somehow dizzying. Janet feels a kind of current, as if time itself, locked in the old minute books, is sweeping backwards under her fingers.

The minutes of April 1908: "The trustees discussed the recent death at Victoria School." No more. Janet reads on through the subsequent meetings of that year and nothing, nothing about the murder, although everything else—including the new toilets—was discussed in detail. She slams the minute book closed.

The Victorians were so bloody euphemistic, so obsessed with façade. Something is left unsaid here, she feels it, something connected to pitiful Thomas. How did Violet Smith describe him? Disgusting. It's the same word the newspapers used to describe Tarpaper Town. Disgusting habits, the editorial said. Why disgusting, another strange turn of phrase?

Janet grabs her purse and drives the fifty miles to Toronto to the provincial archives, arriving forty minutes before closing, but it doesn't take more than twenty minutes to find what she's looking for. It's all there in the court testimony. Thomas' uncle jailed for one year on the charge of procuring, procuring for child prostitution. Poor, poor little boy, no wonder everyone found him *disgusting*. Why did he come to school at all? It was pitiful. How did his schoolmates treat him? She can imagine. No doubt the parents warned their children to stay away from him. No wonder they called him the Yegg Boy. That was probably the mildest of epithets.

And suddenly Janet knows consciously, what she had known subconsciously from the beginning. She knows who killed Thomas.

She thinks of telling Mark the next morning as they walk to the former site of Tarpaper Town, now a dusty waste of weed, sand and bushes, a little east of the main street, between the lake and the train tracks, but, for some reason, she can't speak of it. Of what use is her information? Useless dry stuff, like history itself, like the blowing sand and grit around them and yet—and yet—the murder holds a strange power, filling her mind with mental pictures and making it difficult to concentrate on what Mark is saying.

"The police burned Tarpaper Town down in October, 1939," Mark says, "just after the war started. Security reasons, they said, it being so close to the tracks. There've been many other shack towns in Canada and in the end they always get burned down or bulldozed down, or whatever: Tarpaper Town, Swamp Town, Hobo Jungle, Shanty Town—they're the other side, the shadow side."

Janet remembers the famous Rooster Town in Winnipeg, long destroyed. And after the Second World War, she recalls with shame a poor section of Nipigon labeled D.P. Town.

"Violet Smith says she's glad they burned it down."

"People are always glad." Mark is suddenly fierce. "Do you know how many people lived here, Janet? Three hundred. That's quite a large community when you think that Port Gill had less than 10,000 people at the time."

"Thomas Teasdale lived here," Janet says. "Did you know his uncle was a pimp, a child pimp? Probably pimped out Thomas."

Then Mark says something that makes her really like him. "Oh God, the poor child," he says. "Poor tortured little soul."

Janet feels the Yegg Boy's shadow walk beside her as she enters Violet Smith's primary room at the end of the day. The teacher is cutting coloured letters from construction paper. "Evelyn Carstairs and you became friends?" Janet says.

"Firm, firm friends. Right from my first day."

"Sooner or later, Miss Smith, you must have realized that she murdered Thomas."

"She certainly did not!"

"She stowed him in the cloakroom for the day," Janet says. "At morning recess she came here, to this room, for the usual tea party. She left the child alone in spite of the rule requiring her to stay in the class with him, isn't that right? And when she returned, he was hanging from one of those hooks in the cloakroom. He had the mark on his neck. So she—"

"He hung himself," Violet snaps, tears framing her eyes. "The child hung himself. The other children called him such nasty names. Filthy words! And you are right, my dear. I figured it out too. And eventually Evelyn did tell me. A suicide. Not murder. No! The poor child was a complete outcast. People said he was a prostitute. Not even the Tarpaper Town children were nice to him. We never could decide why he came to school at all. She lifted him up off the hook, but he was dead. He was already dead. The bell was ringing. She panicked."

"And so, she hid the body?" Janet added.

"Of course she did. You have to understand that she was very young, practically a child herself. Sixteen years old. Her class was coming in. She hid the body in her supply cupboard and then, after four o'clock, she went upstairs and she could hear

THE ART OF BURGLARY

them all in the men teachers' room, Mr. Greenwood and the vice principal and that awful Mr. Aitkens who was principal by the time I came; they were always in there so it was easy for her to get the key from the hook in the office and put it back later. The workmen had gone and Mr. Greenwood had already checked the basement and was back upstairs."

"So, she threw the dead child in the pit."

"Yes," says Violet Smith. "Yes, she did. She thought the body would sink and never be found. She didn't realize all those pipes and things ran under the cement."

"All to prevent being fired."

"It's all very well for you to talk," Violet snaps, her voice fierce. "It's a different world for you. We had to toe the line and all our life too. We didn't get to be principal. Not even vice-principal. We didn't get our picture on the wall or the big fancy staff room. We got frozen at yard duty and if we made one mistake we were gone. It didn't matter if that mistake was in school or out. Our lives were the business of every busybody in town in those days. The men could more or less do what they liked. And you listen to this. The men teachers could get married, but we could not. Have you ever even heard of the marriage bar, Miss Marsden?" her voice shakes with bitterness. "I don't suppose you have. Lady teachers were barred from marriage in those days. Automatic termination." She pronounces each syllable. "Think about it. Just think about it."

Janet feels her inner certainties tumbling.

"And after forty-eight years do you know what Evelyn's pension was?" Violet continues, her voice rising into a shout. "Four hundred and sixty-five dollars a month. Four hundred and sixty five dollars." Violet Smith starts to cry. "How she lives on that amount I do not know."

"Lives?" Janet says. "She's still alive?"

"Of course she is. In Pineview Manor. She's ninety now. Her birthday's coming up. I visit her all the time. Sharp as a tack. We're still friends. Always will be."

"Buildings express the conditions of life and the society around them," said the nineteenth century architect, John Root.

How right he was.

The spacious men teachers' room now makes Janet feel sick. She puts her rolls of blueprints in the much smaller lady teachers' room, which is now a supply room, and she gets a chair and sits there for a long time, looking at shelves stacked with boxes of pencils and exercise books. *The past follows us*, she thinks, *unstable as a cloud, twisted as a labyrinth, at its heart unknowable.* She is a woman of the twentieth century, a person ready for the twenty-first century and yet, today, in the persons of Violet Smith and her friend, Evelyn Carstairs, time has folded up like a fan, contracted itself backward to the turn of the century. Janet always considered the early 1900's as ancient, foreign, remote, the property of historians and novelists, but now, suddenly, she has joined an iron chain linked to 1908 and a hanging boy.

Ninety-year-old Miss Evelyn Carstairs was sixteen years old in 1908 and just finishing up her first year of teaching. On her way back to her classroom after the tea party, she finds the Yegg Bay hanging from a coat hook in the cloakroom. The recess bell is ringing. The class will be rushing in. She lifts the child down and then, *then*—and this part Janet didn't tell Violet Smith, but she knows it happened—sixteen-year-old Evelyn Carstairs tightens the kerchief around the child's neck. She tightens hard. *Massive damage to the windpipe.* She has to make sure he is dead. She shoves the body in the supply cupboard. She'll think of a way to get rid of it later.

And pretty Miss Carstairs lived on as a murderer for over seventy years.

"What are you sitting in here for?" Mark is smiling at the door of the supply closet, but his eyes are slits; she wonders if he thinks her a little odd. She stares at him, transfixed. He is now the intruder, the obstacle, a blank part of the labyrinth, another face in the line on the wall downstairs.

"I'm all right," Janet says, trying for balance, for fairness. "I think I'm in mourning for a little boy. How about lunch? I'll try to tell you all about it, although I'm not sure I completely understand it myself."

❖

Bright sun is flooding the greenhouse. Her husband Mark is staring at her and she is staring into space with a small pansy plant dangling from one hand and a small pot of soil in the other.

He says, "If it hadn't been for Thomas Randall Teasdale, we might never have..."

Janet turns away, thinking about his words and wondering why she feels exasperated. She bangs the pansy into the pot. Both of them now old, retired, busy, their lives full of meaning—at least they like to think so. Yet, their involvement in life will last only a comparatively short time more. But to say that this scrap of humanity, this Yegg Boy, is connected to them, that he counts as a person because he helped them find each other...

Oh, Mark, she wants to say, the child was born, suffered, died a horrible death. This was a life that meant nothing or, if it had any meaning at all, what sort of meaning? Surely not that it connected us.

His kindly smile stops her comments. He means well. He always means well. A kindly man, a loving man.

Long ago, she told him everything, even the visit she paid to the nursing home. Summerhill Manor. Why had she gone? Curiosity? To see a ninety-year-old murderer? How foolish. She still feels ashamed. She tries not to think about it.

She remembers only a little, walking through a large room where several very old people were sitting or standing here and there. The nurse led her through another door out to the sun room where Evelyn Carstairs sat alone, deeply asleep. The old woman's head drooped, but Janet could see

THE ART OF BURGLARY

her face was twitching. When the nurse left, Janet stood for a minute, unsure of what to do or even why she was there. As she moved a step closer, she became aware of an odour, not exactly urine or excrement but something thicker, a grainier smell, unpleasantly sour. She stood indecisively. The old woman opened one eye and Janet, with a start, and without thinking, swung around and hurried from the room.

Now, safe in her greenhouse, she touches Mark's hand. His smile is tentative. She knows he loves her. And, she thinks, that counts for a great deal, after all. She sets the potted pansy into its plastic tray. "Let's go in for lunch," she says.

MEMORIES OF A CAJUN NIGHT

The Cajun orchestra, skeining out wild music through the open doors and windows of the dance hall, greeted Loreen and me as we walked through the oak-scented night. A revved-up accordion, fiddle and guitar drowned the noise of cars on the road, the beat of surf beyond the dunes and the laughter of the dancers. Their shoes on the bare boards snapped out a bass line as they flew through a Louisiana two-step.

I met Loreen at the Grand Isle Bird Festival, an annual bird-watching event held every April in this village built precariously on a barrier island south of New Orleans in the Gulf of Mexico.

Y'all's une Canadienne," she said, "so y'all have un vrai bon temps."

Loreen's accent was as thick as molasses and I had to twist my ears into knots to decipher the rolling English mixed with the odd word of French.

The dance hall reminded me of country halls in Northern Ontario. Long and low and open to the warm night, the bar took up one end and the stage for the perspiring musicians the other. Wooden tables circled the dance floor. Loreen introduced me to the ten or twelve people around her table: sisters, cousins, neighbours and another birder who had come for the festival, a former resident of Grand Isle and now a doctor in New Orleans.

"Bienvenue," the doctor said as I sat down beside him. "That's the only French I know."

"English is fine," I said.

"When I was a kid in school, we weren't allowed to speak French," the doctor explained. "My grandparents were fluent, but my parents wouldn't let us kids say one word. They thought it would hold us back in life. Thankfully, things are different now."

I'd heard French was on the upswing in Louisiana. He agreed. His own kids were in French immersion. Last year, he and his family went to a francophone festival in Manitoba and were planning to go to another in Nova Scotia.

The music blasted forth and the doctor and I swung into the two-step. It was surprisingly easy to do, a cross between a polka and a quick foxtrot with some added creative footwork. The hard part was keeping my feet going fast enough to stay in sync with the rhythm. Thankfully, cold beer and Coca-Cola arrived at the table and soon, after a pause to find some breath, everyone was talking to me at once. The doctor wandered over to talk to the musicians.

"Y'all try the crawdads yet?" said Loreen's cousin, a large woman who was a lightning-fast dancer.

"No, but the shrimp we had last night was wonderful."

"We Cajuns survived by eating everything," said Loreen. "In the 1700's, when they dropped us on this sand spit—because that's all Grand Isle is—we had to eat everything we could catch: alligator, raccoon, possum, snakes."

The others took up the list: "turtles, armadillo, crabs, squirrel, snails, doves..."

"Even robins" said the doctor who returned to the table. "But everything we cooked, we cooked with French flair. So now, we eat some of the best cuisine in the world."

Had he really said they ate robins? I was appalled. He must have seen the look on my face.

"That's right, robins. My grandpa caught them in nets at spring migration. He chopped off their little heads, reached into the cavity with two fingers and hauled out the breasts. Then he threw the rest away. It takes a lot of robin breasts to make a meal for a family." He grinned. "Don't worry, we don't eat songbirds any more—just watch them."

The bandleader stepped to the mike. "I hear we have a Canadian in our midst," he said, to my intense surprise and embarrassment. "So, welcome to Grand Isle. Welcome to the bird festival. Now here's a song for our visitor from a long lost place." The old Quebec tune of *Vive la Canadienne* shot like sheet lightning around the hall and everyone was on their feet. I danced with one of Loreen's elderly cousins, doing a maniac two-step, interspersed with creative jive dance moves. Several people were singing the chorus:

>*Vive La Canadienne*
>*Et ses jolis yeux doux.*

THE ART OF BURGLARY

When the music stopped and I retrieved my breath, I called out, "Thank you, thank you everyone." I bowed left and right. "Merci, tout le monde. Merci beaucoup."

It was a magical moment in my life, to feel so strongly the ancient connection between Canada and Louisiana, a connection I had not seriously considered until then.

HORSES ON THE RIO GRANDE

"Janet," A whiney voice in the blackness of the tent. "Janet."

I open my tired eyes. "What now, Barbie?"

"I hear the horses. I'm sure they're out there. And I have to wee wee. I'm afraid to go outside."

Wee wee. A grown woman, mid-twenties, maybe older, saying wee wee. It's ridiculous. "So you want me to go with you, right?"

"Please, Janet. Pretty please."

Damn. I unzip my sleeping bag. The desert air is chill. I fumble for the flashlight and aim it at the tent zipper so Barbie can get herself into the open air. "Put your shoes on," I say. "You don't want to step on a cactus."

Moonlight touches the tops of the tents, slides across the wide water of the Rio Grande, sketches the line of canoes on the bank, and outlines the dark hills on the Mexican side. From upstream comes the whinny of horses, the wild horses of the Big Bend of the Rio Grande. Occasionally, during the past week on the river, we glimpsed small herds of the heavy bellied, piebald animals. They raised their heads to stare at us, their eyes mild with a blank curiosity. Sometimes, they would whinny, stamp and turn, splashing along the shallows and

THE ART OF BURGLARY

disappearing behind the stands of carrizo cane that line the banks. They never came near our campsites and, our guide, Elizabeth Beauville, assures us they're shy of people.

"Why is it so stony?" Barbie's stumbling, her feet half in and half out of her pink sneakers. "Why didn't we camp at that place with the nice sand?

"You can't camp at the mouth of a side canyon. Rain far up in the hills could send down a flash flood."

"Ooh, yuck," Barbie stops. "Look at all the horse droppings."

I swivel the flashlight. Dry horse turds the size and shape of Frisbees dot the area in front of us.

"Old stuff," I say. "Good fuel."

"Y'all so brave Janet. I would never pick up those icky things like you do. You make such great fires."

I almost replied, *and you, Miss Southern Belle, do dick-all, except change your clothes and put on make-up.* Instead, I pull her to one side before she walks into a barrel cactus. I'm getting very tired of babysitting Barbara Jean Rawlins. On our first day, Elizabeth suggested her as my canoe partner, the idea being I would brush up her canoe skills and review the rudiments of white water. Elizabeth took on the other newbie, a large and capable looking sixteen-year-old girl. The remaining two canoes are manned by seasoned canoeists, Texan gals, old hands on the river, who'd been on many trips together.

As I wait for Barbie to finish on the other side of a clump of tall carrizo, I wonder if I can put up with her much longer. She's a fair canoeist who knows the major strokes, but, whenever the river picks up speed, she seems to fall into a doze, perhaps mesmerized by the roar of the water and the dark colours of the roiling current. The Rio Grande, placid and lazy along much of its length, can turn dangerous, taking on speed as it runs downhill, squeezing into narrow canyons, flinging itself against red cliffs, and, at every turn and twist, sending brown water roaring up the rock walls in dizzying waves.

Yesterday afternoon, going through a narrow canyon, I had to scream at her. "Barbie! Wake up and back paddle, goddamn it!"

In the stern, I was aiming for a back ferry, a move to keep the canoe at an angle to the current so that the boat would not be slammed into the side of the cliff. In the very fast water, I needed all my strength to set the angle and hold it in place. The bow person is supposed to back paddle like mad to move us across the current, but Barbie just sat there, her paddle across her lap.

"Back paddle, you idiot or we'll both drown," I screamed over the noise of the water. Barbie's shoulders gave a little shake and at last she set her paddle in the water. "Put your damn back into it." We shot out of the canyon with inches to spare.

Elizabeth met us on the bank. Her voice was gentle. "What happened Barbie? Why weren't you paddling?"

"Janet yelled at me."

"Before that, honey, you were just sitting there like a little ole' ornament."

"I don't know. I was scared." She sounded like a ten year old.

"We have at least three canyons to go. Janet's a strong canoeist, but she can't navigate these narrow spots without your help."

Barbie sniffled. She looked at me. "You swore at me."

I took a deep breath and stared at this child-woman, leaning on her paddle, staring into space. I tried to remove my anger from my voice. "Sorry," I said. "I'm a Canadian. We swear," *and*, I mentally added, *especially before we die.*

Safe on the bank, Barbie looked as cool as if she were setting out to the church picnic. On the other hand, my heart was convulsing. She had no idea of the danger she'd put us in.

On a smooth shallow stretch of river, we again practiced back paddling and draw strokes. Again, I explained that when the river runs fast and the canyon turns, the current could slam the canoe straight into a cliff. I drew a picture in the sand of a boat doing a back ferry. "This is how you avoid being flipped into the water because when that happens, the current could hold you against the wall and, if it does, you'll drown." She looked bored. Her mind seemed far away. I sensed she did not believe me. This gal had obviously led a princess life. Nothing bad could possibly happen to her.

"Are you still game, Janet?" Elizabeth asked me later in her soft Texan drawl. "Can you carry on with her?" Elizabeth, small, blond, curly-haired, had been guiding for several years. She had written the book about canoeing the Rio Grande. I knew she was worried.

I considered. "I think so. I'll just keep reminding her when we get near a canyon."

Now, outside in the first touch of dawn, I smell the sweet desert breeze carrying perfume from unseen flowers. A touch of sun edges the Mexican hills. This is beauty time, when the entire landscape glows colour: apricot, rose, rust, dark-banded purple and gold. Once the sun is high, and it moves there quickly, the land sinks back into everyday brown until sunset starts the show again.

Barbie steps out from behind the cane. "Look across the river," she says, her voice soft.

A man is standing on the Mexican shore.

"An illegal?" I feel a shiver of fear. Would a man who'd already walked through miles of desert be desperate for food or water, desperate enough to rob? Kill? "Could he be dangerous?"

"No, no," she answers. "He isn't carrying a pack. He's here for another reason."

The man is very still, staring at our tents. Barbara and I are partly hidden by the tall cane. He carries a coiled rope over one shoulder. The soft whinny of the horses upstream has him angle his head in their direction.

Barbie steps to the edge of the water. "Hola!" she calls.

I grab her by the arm. "What are you doing?"

The man answers in Spanish and the two shout back and forth.

"He's coming over to get a few horses, is all," Barbie says. "I told him that's all right. We're no danger to him. Just canoeists."

A horse and rider appear on the far hill. I slide my feet backward in surprise and fear.

"Don't worry, Janet. It's his friend."

The rider leads a second horse. The man on the shore swings up into its saddle. The two move slowly to the river's edge, enter the water and quietly head upstream.

"He says this is the best place to cross," Barbie says.

"Is it stealing, to take the horses?"

"I don't know. Maybe. This is a national park so I'm thinking they're protected. But you know, the Mexicans are poor, a lot of them."

Elizabeth comes out to join us. "Horse thieves," she says.

Even in the soft sand and mud by the river, we can hear the thuds of hooves. "Yip! yip! Hi! Hi!" yell the riders as they emerge from the unending cane, swinging their ropes, three riderless horses thundering ahead of them.

One minute, the captured animals are coming towards us, eyes rolling, manes and tails flying, snorting in fear and a few seconds later, they all turn into the river, water snapping under their hooves. On the far bank they become silhouettes in the newly risen sun: five horses, two riders, the dark snaking ropes. They disappear around a fold of hill.

"What will they do with them?"

"Pasture them somewhere. Then kill them and sell the meat," Elizabeth says.

I ponder this as I eat my chili and tortilla breakfast. Such beautiful animals. The other members of the party seem unsurprised by the story. "I wonder if the park rangers keep a count," the sixteen-year-old says. The others shrug.

My thoughts turn to the riddle that is Barbie.

Inside our tent, as we are packing our kit, I say, "That was a smart move, talking to that Mexican. I didn't know what he was up to and I was pretty nervous."

"Oh, most Mexicans are nice, actually. I figured out they were after horses. Perfect area, a shallow ford, lots of hoof prints on the far shore, lots of horse droppings around. They've been here before, I expect. Our tents must have been a surprise."

"Thanks," I say. "I'm sorry I swore at you yesterday. Maybe we'll have a better run today."

"Yesterday, I wanted to kill myself, Janet."

What the hell? "Yesterday, in the canyon?"

She nods.

"And why? And also take me with you. Thanks so much." My voice rose, half in anger, half in fear.

"No, no. I was thinking of jumping out."

"Much good that would do. In that current, we'd have gone over and then wrapped against the cliff." It takes all my willpower to shut up, calm myself and moderate my tone. "Well, I'm glad you changed your mind," I say carefully.

"My husband died."

I look at her. *She's married?* I thought she was single. All I can say is "When?"

THE ART OF BURGLARY

"Three weeks ago. He was twenty-eight. Liver cancer. He died in a week."

Oh damn. I'm caught off guard. I sit back in surprise and stare at her. "I'm so sorry," I finally say. "So then, you wanted to die too?"

"Not at first. I thought this trip would heal me. Help me get over it. It didn't work. All this sand, eating on the ground, using horse stuff for fuel. My clothes are filthy. I'm filthy. My hair is full of sand. I'm all sand, a sand person, a mud person, just going down a stupid, ugly, polluted river. I should just die too. Get it over quick. He's gone, so why not me too?"

I reach for her hand. "Still, you didn't do it."

"That horrible water, just brute ugly, I couldn't." She pauses as I move to sit beside her, put an arm around her shoulders. I'm out of my depth, not knowing the right words, but I'm going to try.

"They took the young horses, the most beautiful ones," she says. "They'll die too. So I think now, I think, I can't..."

Her voice turns into sobs. I hug her tighter, drop my cheek on her blond hair. "I'm so sorry," I say again.

"I can't add to it," she says. "Death, I mean." I wait, feeling her sobs ease down. "Don't tell anyone, please Janet, please. Especially Elizabeth. Promise, please."

I hesitate for only a second. Do I have a choice? The only way out of here is by canoe. I must have this young woman's cooperation; my life may depend on it and so I make the promise.

"Tomorrow we get to a big hot spring," I say. "We'll bathe, wash our hair. You'll feel better."

We take down the tent in silence, add it to the Duluth pack. For the first time she helps, heaving the pack onto her back and heads to the canoe. "We got married three months ago," she says.

How can I answer? I just say, "Ah, Barbie." I feel tears on my cheeks.

I walk with her, carrying our daypacks. The sun is high enough to turn the world sandy brown again. Dragonflies crisscross the water. The air is flat with an edge of heat. Far off, I can hear the shushing sound of the next canyon.

The others are loading up, almost set to go. I push our canoe out and hold it as Barbie scrambles nimbly over the packs into the bow seat. She tucks her day back into the point of the bow and takes up her paddle, pushing the blade into the sandy bottom to hold the boat steady in the placid water.

Elizabeth gives me the thumbs up. She calls to Barbie. "How y'all doing? Ready for the day?"

"Fine," Barbie says without turning her head. "I'll be fine."

Elizabeth and I exchange looks. We'll be first in line today and this is comforting, even though I know there's little the others can do if the current overwhelms us. I set my daypack behind the stern seat. Bending forward, hands ahead holding the gunnels, I wade a couple of steps into the shallows before swinging my legs into the canoe.

"Okay, Barbara," I call to her. "I'm ready."

We push off into the river.

A CEREMONY TO INITIATE
A SWEAT LODGE

I walk along a dark evening path cutting through a field of snow on a moonless Northern Ontario night in mid-March. I am slower than the others, and they patiently wait for me. They know the arthritis in my elderly spine sometimes knots my back and slows me down.

The path leads to a feisty bonfire, flames leaping inside a miniature tipi made of stout logs. A ring of fat granite stones holds the structure in place. Several benches, some with cushions, create a circle for the participants, a dozen or so people in winter parkas and toques, big boots, plain or fancy mittens. We sit or stand in silence, waiting for the ceremony to begin, our faces rosy in the dancing light. Most are Indigenous, but I am not.

Emma, an Anishinaabe Elder, short and stout in her puffy winter jacket and snow pants, arranges items on a bench. She carefully places a shallow circular drum, a large scooped shell, a long wooden box, a cup of water, a basket of tobacco, and another basket of tiny bundles side by side.

We watch in silence as overhead dark blue shades into black, slowly embellished by pinprick stars. Across the fields of snow, I see only the silhouettes of spruce against an awakening sky.

The Elder explains the ceremony. She says she learned it from her grandmother, who lived to be over 100 years old, who learned from her grandmother, who learned it from her grandmother. "I follow what I was taught," she says.

Picking up a basket, she presents each of us with a small piece of cedar leaf and a tiny cloth bundle containing tobacco. "You can put these items on the fire," she explains, "or keep them to bring home, or, if you like, put them on the rocks in the sweat lodge."

Betsy and Shannon arrive with a shovel and a hoe to rake three rocks from the fire. "These rocks are the grandfathers," Emma says. One by one, the rocks, glowing like magical eggs, are pushed into the shovel and carried away into the darkness.

"First we do the ceremony here at the fire," Emma explains, "and after that we go in small groups to look at the new sweat lodge." At her bench, she lights some tobacco previously placed inside the large scooped shell. I look into the dark beyond the fire, trying to find the sweat lodge, but I cannot see it.

Instead, I am surrounded by a curtain of black silk pulsing in the moving light from the flames. I'm enclosed by dark, relaxed, and yet, at the same time, my every sense has quickened. I taste the sweet wood smoke, hear the crackling grumble of the fire, smell the winter world hovering behind my back, sense invisible threads looping me to the others.

THE ART OF BURGLARY

"You bathe in the smoke because it's like water," Emma says. "Think of washing your face with it." From the long box, she removes an eagle feather. She walks around the circle holding the shell and, with a graceful circular motion of her hand, she uses the feather to waft the smoke from the tobacco toward each of us in turn. As she moves, she prays in the Anishinaabe language, a prayer of thanks. Next, she takes up the cup of water. "Water is the most important thing, and, without it, you would be no more." She sprinkles a few drops on the ground. "The ground on which you stand is important, too, and so is the sky."

She hands me a rattle, a hollow cylinder with a deer antler handle. She also gives one to Mary who is standing beside me and to some of the others. We shake the rattles, which, I think, are made from gourds filled with dried seeds. The sound is light and pleasant as it joins with Emma's drum. I'm hypnotized by the merging of sounds: rattles, drum, fire. I experiment a little, shifting the rattle slightly to take on different tones, blending them to the soft shaking sounds around me. I feel sad when we stop.

"The earth is the womb. Once, the Great Mother carried many people in her womb," Emma says, and the words nudge me back into my own history. In half a breath, I recall my awe and terror as my daughter emerged from my own womb and then my own anxiety when her body produced children of her own. And then, they had babies in their turn. I squeeze my eyes together, searching for understanding, but the thought-image vanished.

Instead, I see Emma holding out her hand to ten-year-old Dawn. The two, Elder and child, walk the path to the far field using a flashlight to light the way. It's so dark their shapes disappear into the wall of night that surrounds us. Only a dot of light moves, disappears, and after a few minutes, shines again as the two return. Emma then takes others in groups of three. Finally, it's my turn. About ten steps away from the fire, I am able to make out the tipi shape and, as I get nearer, I see the exterior of the tipi and the shape of someone holding the door open.

The triangular entrance is very low. I have to get down on one knee and try to move forward, difficult for me. As instructed, I enter and move to the left. The interior is surprising, a separate structure, rounded in shape, a high dome held together with strong poplar struts bound and knotted with strips of cloth. I cannot discern the interior skin of the inner lodge; only that it's lively with our shadows.

In the centre, the three grandfather stones glow in the small fire, and once more I am touched lightly by an awareness too quick to grasp: grandmother, mother, daughters, granddaughters, great-granddaughters.

I sit for a minute and then stand—the dome is high enough—and walk around the glowing heart, moving to the left and then out the door. The entrance is so low, I have to slide out on my bottom. Shannon is waiting outside to pull me to my feet. I am helped into the night and back to the fire.

THE ART OF BURGLARY

Emma hands everyone a handful of loose tobacco and suggests we give a good yell and toss it on the fire. "This will help drive away your fears." I let out a weak *ki-yi* as I toss in my tobacco, but the teen-agers present shout and howl like dawn wolves.

I search within myself to find my fears. My chronic unease about my arthritis surfaces along with my persistent worry that, one day, I will become completely disabled, rendered powerless, mentally and physically, in the grasp of this cruel disease.

I reach for the tiny cedar and tobacco bundle in my pocket and hold it tightly. I will not toss it on the fire but bring it home as a reminder. I close my eyes and listen to the teen-age wolves baying at the night sky and laughing. "I need to be strong for the future," I say to whatever spirit surrounds me. I open my eyes and hope the anxieties of old age are dancing away in the rising sparks.

As we walk to the nearby house for a cup of tea and the potluck meal, I am overwhelmed by gratitude towards Emma who invited me, a non-Indigenous person, to participate.

Now, months later, I am still aware from time to time of the old anxieties, but, somehow, they have become linked to a star-dotted sky, rising sparks, teen-agers shouting and a tipi just visible in the snow.

THE MOST BEAUTIFUL BREASTS
IN THUNDER BAY

"It picks up the pink in the lawn chairs," said Barbara pointing to a minuscule dot in the plastic plates. "Bamboo is so post-mo this year and sets off the outdoor concept of Lake Superior so well. And I just knew these paper napkins would be a perfect match for the patio umbrella…" Janet felt the accustomed light and familiar annoyance and she longed to change the subject.

Barbara continued. "Walking into the Superstore, I saw the tablecloth at once. The exact same shade of pink, a miracle. And handmade stitching…"

Janet could remember when Barbara had been a baby called Pudgy. Now, however, Pudgy was a matron in an ironed white shirt and shorts, placing little clips around the table so the cloth would not flap away in the breeze romping across the deck from Lake Superior.

"I heard something interesting," Janet said. "An idea for a new style of summer day camp—an Indigenous day camp with non-Indigenous kids too. The emphasis would be on the outdoors and stories, songs, and drumming. Cool eh?"

Pudgy looked blank, and more than blank, bored and a little alarmed, as if she, Janet, at sixty-six years of age, had finally succumbed to dementia. Pudgy's own kids were in their teens and her expression said that her interest in children's day camps was zero. That was when Janet realized, with a shock, that Pudgy did not understand the purpose of her story—or any of her stories. This brought her an unpleasant snap of self-realization.

I tell her stories all the time, she thought, *and she never gets the point*. For an instant, Janet saw herself as the old hanger-on who had to be invited to the family gatherings whether they wanted her or not—the tiresome old body with the pointless remarks, the Judith Hearne of Thunder Bay.

Off balance, Janet turned toward the lake just as the wind swooped through the birches, whipped under the edge of the tablecloth flipping a snowstorm of plastic clips onto the deck and down through the cracks between the boards.

Janet did not join the scrabble for the clips. Instead she watched the velvet foam-speckled breakers roar into the beach. *All the food will be blown away*, she thought maliciously, *and we will end up rushing around to save the damn placemats and the matching napkins.*

Nevertheless, once the cloth was again secured, she felt impelled to go on. "When we were kids at church camp," she ventured, hoping her words would break through and resurrect the old ways of thinking, "we had Indian Days and dressed up with poster paint on our faces and went around saying 'ugh' to each other." Janet shook her head ruefully, but Pudgy still looked blank. "Racist, of course. Unfortunately, we didn't think in those terms. Now this type of day camp will be an authentic cultural experience and so, good for…" Her voice trailed away. It was obvious that Pudgy did not give a shit.

When car noises sounded from the driveway, the younger woman looked visibly relieved. The newcomers came bearing covered dishes for the potluck that would start as soon as Pudgy's parents arrived. Pudgy started in again. "Take a look at these paper napkins I found," she said to one of the women guests. "They absolutely tie together the plates and glasses."

"Hello, Ms. Fortier," said a newcomer, Pudgy's friend and strangely enough, Rick's son. "Would you like a beer or something? Don't get up, I'll get it."

Janet shook her head. She still was smarting from the realization that she was a bore. She smiled hello at everyone, stood, and walked down to the beach.

Once, a long time ago, when Pudgy was a roly-poly infant and Janet was in her forties, she and a half dozen friends arrived at this same summer camp, then a smaller building, a three room shack actually, the only cottage on this secluded cove in Lake Superior called Caribou Bay. She and her friends were on a summer outing to ease the stress in their lives with a sauna and a swim.

THE ART OF BURGLARY

That was also the day Janet first noticed that her breasts had grown. Also, that they floated. She looked down at them, white and blue veined and floating. One of the biggest surprises of her life. Who knew breasts could float? It was true they seemed to be growing larger the past year, perhaps because she'd given up wearing a bra. It wasn't that she gained weight; she was still the same 130 pounds with the same floppy childbirth belly, but, for some reason, her breasts had just taken off.

She had been the first one out of the sauna and for a minute she had the lake to herself. Now Nora came pounding out, flashing naked down the dock, cannonballing off the end.

Nora, long and white, floating on her back, paddled towards her, black hair streaming and said, "You know, Janet, you've got the most beautiful breasts in Thunder Bay. Everybody noticed in the sauna."

Nora's own breasts were small, dark-nippled with hair around them, emphatic punctuation for a body lanky and athletic.

"They float," said Janet and showed her.

Nora was entranced. "Beautiful," she said, "far out fuckin' beautiful."

Stuart came charging out next in a flurry of powerful muscles, hesitated at the edge of the dock, teetered, and jumped to the accompaniment of the women's catcalls.

Janet ducked under, swam a bit, let her feet find the rippled sand and stood to let her breasts float again as Stuart surfaced. She hoped he would notice. Graham, Nora's partner, heavy and hairy, barrelled across the dock and then Gordon and Lucy, two small perfectly-formed human beings, ran together holding hands. Gordon's sister, Gwen, who did not like to swim, sat on the beach holding Lucy's baby, Pudgy, who was naked except for a kerchief cap.

Janet breathed in the smell of water, wood smoke from the sauna and the scent of spruce forest. She lifted her new breasts to the sun. But, there was Rick, standing naked on the shore, eyeing her with his sarcastic expression. In embarrassment, she swam under the surface and then rushed to get a towel from the old overturned boat.

Later they sat on towels on the beach and argued. Rick smoked a cigarette and expounded on the Marxist theory of art. Graham talked about the co-op bookstore and Nora said they were all crazy, the most important thing was an alternative school, and someone else mentioned the proposed day care, and someone else talked about a gardening cooperative, and Lucy said she and Gordon met a mechanic and wouldn't it be great if they could start a co-op garage and save everyone a lot of money, and Rick said these small attempts at co-op enterprises just sucked energy from the revolution, and Stuart said, "I don't believe in your fucking revolution."

And so on.

The voices nipped along as vigorous as the light bouncing on the waves, tripping from topic to topic, sparkling, funny and sharp.

THE ART OF BURGLARY

Pudgy was carried inside to be fed and then brought back to swim. Although the water was Lake Superior icy, she did not protest but flapped her chubby arms as her father held her in a swimming position. Back in the sauna, Janet sat in the top row of naked people, who were now telling stories. Rick told them about an Indigenous girl who, one night, was hit by a car while she was crossing a parking lot. The fifteen-year-old got no settlement because the lawyer convinced the judge she was drunk and lurched into the vehicle.

They listen gravely, swept with sadness. They told similar stories of their own, what they knew of racism, how they had encountered it in their small northern city.

Janet put Pudgy on her lap and bathed her in cool water from the plastic pan and, to change the mood, recited to her. "The owl and the pussycat went to sea in a beautiful pea green boat." Pudgy's dark Goya eyes stared at her unwinkingly as she talked.

Everyone laughed as Gordon continued with Kipling. "If you, Pudgy, can keep your head when all about you are losing theirs and blaming it on you..." The baby's dark eyes followed her father's every word.

It was getting too hot for the infant, so her mother took her out to dip her in the lake. Rick threw a dipper of water on the stones and, in a quick, sadistic move, tossed a cold splash at the line of people on the top shelf.

"You bastard," Graham said.

"I learned *The Lady of Shallot* in grade seven and recited it at the church picnic," Janet said. "Memorization of poetry opens the creative channels."

"No one should memorize poems," countered Nora. "I hated it. None of that in our alternative school." They argued amiably about this and about the South African ambassador's visit and whether it was worthwhile to picket, as some of them had planned to do the next day.

"Useless," said Rick. "You've got to connect it to the entire struggle, the use of racism to foster the capitalist system."

"Oh, for fuck sake," Stuart said.

Later, Janet drove Nora and Graham back to town in her old Datsun. Nora let her wet black hair fall over the back of the front seat and Graham, sitting in the back, stroked it.

"I told Janet she has the most beautiful breasts in Thunder Bay," Nora said. "I'm right, right?"

"They're beautiful, Janet." Graham was smiling at her in the mirror, just a pleasant smile, not a seductive one and continued to stroke Nora's hair.

Since Janet's two girls were at Science Camp for the weekend, she could accept their invitation for dinner. They lived in an old part of the city, a raddled downtown street of cheap hotels, marginal businesses and drunken yells in the middle of the night. They had four high-ceilinged rooms above a second-hand furniture store and the living room, almost a perfect twelve-foot cube according to Graham, had been painted a pale orange. He likened it to being inside a real orange. The couple's

THE ART OF BURGLARY

bicycles were leaning against one wall. The only other items in the room were five or six huge blue cushions made by Nora and a tiny television sitting in the middle of the floor.

In the kitchen, they ate a hastily assembled stir-fry and Nora's homemade bread and talked heatedly about the philosophy of the alternative school and then moved into the living room with their mint teas. The talk moved to their jobs.

"I'm sure I can get back with the school board part-time in September," said Nora, who'd been working at the psychiatric hospital since the cutbacks. "I'm just waiting for the call. Part-time and I can work on the alternative school. Full-time work and I run out of energy."

"How's the library and ol' Roger?" Graham asked Janet. He was referring to her new boss.

"Do you know what he said yesterday?" Janet sipped her tea, lining up the words she'd memorized for the occasion. She used a sonorous tone. "Some of our functions will be realigned to enhance the district operation."

Laughing, Nora fell back on her cushions. "I predict another reshuffle," she said in a spooky fortune-teller voice. "Either that or," she makes a *voila!* gesture with her hand, "strategic planning! Strategic planning is on stream."

Janet laughed to hear her boss's favourite expressions. "The mission statement is now on stream," she said. "You should've seen Roger's face when I read my first version. "Our job is to lend books to people. He looked even more constipated

203

than usual. He insisted I work in the word *stakeholders* somehow."

Then Janet told them a story. When Roger started at the library a month ago, he announced a staff meeting after work. "I'm a part-timer," one woman said. "Will I get paid extra for staying on?"

Roger looked surprised and—you could almost hear the cogs behind the massive bald head—said, "No, part-time staff can leave," and every one got up except Janet.

"He'd no idea our branch was staffed by casuals," Janet said.

"Too bad he doesn't know you have the most beautiful breasts in Thunder Bay," said Graham. "Maybe I should write him an anonymous letter. That would perk ol' Rog up."

Now, thirty-five years later, watching the waves of Caribou Bay, Janet thought of those chipped plates, the mugs bought second-hand or acquired from here and there, the lack of a serving spoon so they had to improvise and dish out the stir fry using a potato masher. Graham ate his food with a teaspoon. She thought of swimming nude, something she had not done for a long time, and the naked conversations on the beach.

Eventually, Lucy and Gordon went to work in Winnipeg and passed the camp on to Pudgy. Pudgy's husband tore down the shack and built a rustic six-room cottage, complete with indoor plumbing, electricity, and a massive deck. When

THE ART OF BURGLARY

Janet had gone inside, she'd not been surprised to find copies of *Cottage Life*, *People* magazine and *Vogue* on the coffee table.

Now she walked to the end of the dock, turning back once to look at the shiny cottage, the guests on the deck—most of them unknown to her—and the large houses surrounding the cove.

Rick's son walked across the sand holding a beer towards her. He was a handsome young man, a black-haired James Dean and thus exactly like his father at the same age.

"Do you miss your dad?" Janet asked.

"The crustiest bugger that ever walked the earth? Yeah, I miss him a lot."

"It was wonderful what you and Alma did—taking him into your house to die."

"We got the hospital bed and everything. Set it up in the living room. I even let him smoke—what the hell, why not? I actually held him when he was dying." The young man turned his face away into the roaring wind. "Just another disappointed old Commie smoking himself to death."

"So he was still a Communist to the end?"

"No, no, not to the end. It frittered out and, after the Berlin Wall, he stopped talking about it. Most likely he was the last Commie in Thunder Bay."

"But do you know, Ms. Fortier," he continued, "what he really was? He was a lover. He loved you guys. The nights he couldn't sleep, he told me lots about the old times. You guys did everything. Ban the bomb, Kamchaka, anti-war demos, God, I wish I'd been around. Life was so intense then. All I do now is go to the Waterkeeper meetings and, man, they're pretty dull."

"We had this fantastic feeling we were winning," Janet said. She stopped. She knew he couldn't follow her train of thought.

"Do you know what he said about you?"

"What?" Janet said.

"You had the most beautiful breasts in Thunder Bay."

She threw back her head and laughed. "I loved him too," she said, suddenly switching to tears. "I loved him very much." They stood for a minute, arms around each other.

She walked by herself to the end of the beach and back. She realized she was, once again, in mourning. She was not even sure where her grief was focused. She was not mourning the past: the many saunas, the picnics, the arguments and talks and parties, the baseball and broomball games. These were sweet memories. Nor was it the projects, so many of them failures, although a few had lasted a long time: the co-op clothing store (short lived), a food network (still going), co-op gardens and businesses that failed, a leather shop, a poster shop and a vegetarian restaurant. The co-op bookstore closed a few years ago. The alternative school never happened. And all the demos—Take Back the Night, Ban the Bomb, Get Out of Vietnam and dozens more—surely they'd done some good. And, she thought ruefully, the most beautiful breasts brought her no permanent lover to replace her long gone and half-forgotten husband.

THE ART OF BURGLARY

Anything seemed possible then and everything seemed connected, the creation of a community, the eschewing of consumerism, the buying of one's dishes at the Sally Ann.

Then she realized the source of her sadness. It had nothing to do with the activities. It was the people, the fact you'd hear on a Tuesday that the South African ambassador was coming to town the following Sunday, make some calls and have three hundred people out on the street in front of his hotel. Most of these old-timers had moved away. The gay guys had moved as a contingent to Toronto; others, like Pudgy's parents, Gordon and Lucy, had gone to Winnipeg in search of jobs.

And now this generation, they do not tell stories, she thought. *They can't even decipher a story.*

She put the beer bottle on the dock, moved her bare feet into the brutally cold water of Lake Superior and, fully clothed in pants and shirt, floundered in and dove. She swam a few strokes into the waves that were now roaring maniacally. She stood, dizzy with cold to see Gordon and Lucy walking down the path. Their visit from Winnipeg was the point of the party. Janet was filled with love and gratitude that they were there. When she ran to the beach, they tossed her the towel they'd brought down for her.

"I heard an interesting thing when we stopped for gas," said Gordon.

"Wait a minute before you tell the story," said Lucy. "Janet must be cold."

"Not at all," Janet said.

DANGEROUS LIAISONS

Surprisingly, the air seemed much warmer in the evening. The day had been chilly, but, as I walked back to my camper, beads of sweat were running down my back under my T-shirt. I stopped on the camper steps to listen to the rhythm of surf across the dune that separated me from the Gulf of Mexico. Tiny stars prickled the inky sky. It was January 2003 at St. Joseph State Park in the Florida Panhandle.

It was warmer inside the camper. But it wasn't until I undressed for bed that I understood the heat was originating from my body and not the weather. A pink circle, four inches in diameter, was inscribed on the skin of my left thigh. In the centre sat a second circle coloured a dark glowing red. In the middle, a tiny black dot created a pattern like a target at a rifle range.

When I put my hand over the bull's eye, I could feel heat emanating into my palm. The entire design was slightly raised and seemed to vibrate with a faint pulse. Obviously I had been bitten by something. I guessed it was a spider. Four years ago, on my 65th birthday, I got a spider bite on a canoe trip. A circular red welt rose up on the cheek of my ass. The doctor said it would go away in a day

THE ART OF BURGLARY

or two and it did. So, now, in Florida, and on my own, I determined to ignore it and head for bed.

At dawn and out bird watching as usual, I felt hot and dizzy as I stumbled through the palmetto behind the camp. I turned back to my vehicle. *Time to take action.* I had never been to an American hospital before and the small plain building in the city of St. Joseph was unprepossessing, a basic one-storey, windowless box covered with scabby pink paint. In the shabby lobby, orange plastic chairs circled the worn linoleum. In spite of the early hour, a dozen patients lolled about. I presented myself at the small counter and flipped up the hem of my shorts so the nurse could get a good look at my fancy thigh.

"Oh, my God!" she said. "Oh, my God!" She ran around the counter, grabbed me by the elbow and hustled me across the room, past the startled patients, through a set of double swinging doors, and down a short corridor into a small consulting room. She thrust me inside and then rushed away.

I had barely sat down when the doctor appeared, stopped inside the door and stared at my leg. I was coyly holding up the hem of the shorts. He was a handsome young man with a neat reddish beard. He threw himself on his knees in front of me and leaned his face a few inches from my thigh.

"I don't like this," he said. "I don't like this at all." Springing to his feet, he rushed out, returning a few seconds later with the nurse. A minute later, down came the shorts and a needle shot into my butt.

"You've been bitten by a brown recluse spider," he told me, and then asked several questions about what I was doing in Florida, where I was camping and so on. At the same time, he was writing out prescriptions.

"Get some spider spray and go over your camper especially in the crevices. Better bundle up the bedclothes and take them to the laundry. The spider may be hiding in the covers or lurking in the cracks. Or you could've been bitten outside, perhaps at the picnic table. This spider hides away, hence the name, brown recluse."

Drops of my perspiration dripped on the prescription paper. I was getting dizzier by the minute. "Anything else?" I said.

"Wash the area with soap and hot water. Wash it a lot. There's a danger of necrosis." I stood up unsteadily, unsure of the meaning of necrosis. It sounded very unpleasant.

"And if you feel your throat swelling shut, or your tongue swelling and your airway closing, come right to the hospital."

"Right oh," I said, and wove my way outside and around the corner to the drugstore.

I asked the pharmacist for a glass of water so that I could take the two pills immediately, but, when she heard the words *brown recluse*, she looked so stricken I was sorry I mentioned it. Several customers clustered around to hear my story and stare at my thigh. Then clutching a large aerosol can of spider spray, I wobbled forth to battle.

THE ART OF BURGLARY

I drove the truck camper a block to the laundromat and parked in the lot across the street. Then I stripped my bed, shoving everything into a green plastic garbage bag. After tossing the mattress on the floor, I held my breath as I sprayed the entire camper and left it to marinate in the foul smelling vapour. Once I got the bedclothes into the washer, I went into the restroom, washed and soaped my leg and covered the area with Mecca Ointment. I have a lot of faith in Mecca Ointment, and, if necrosis meant what I thought it did—gangrene—I was counting on the old-fashioned Canadian remedy, one which had cleared up infections in the past.

Driving is not easy when you are dizzy from fever and psychological shock. When I got back to the campground, I sprayed the camper again, closed it up and then sat outside at the picnic table, my book unopened, dripping sweat and watching the tops of the palms sway against the sky. Suddenly, I remembered the doctor's words about the picnic table. Grabbing the spider spray, I leaned under it, spraying every tiny crack. I moved to a lawn chair and fell into a doze, getting up every once in a while to check the smell inside the camper, take another vitamin C, boil water and wash my leg, and then slather on the Mecca.

The woman in the next campsite came over to check on me. Apparently my story had gone round. She was a nurse. "If you feel your airway swelling, come get me at once and I'll drive you to the hospital," she said. When she asked if there was anything she could get for me, I requested a cup of boiling water for tea. She looked puzzled. Tea in Florida means iced tea, but she kindly brought me what I needed. Psychologically, Canadian Red Rose tea is the answer.

By evening, I felt better. I phoned my daughter Suzanne at home and she laughed when I told her the spider story. "Put on Mecca Ointment," she said. A half hour later, she phoned back. "The kids looked up *brown recluse* on the internet," she said. "People get gangrene. They have to amputate. They found this guy's diary online. They're really upset. We'll come and get you."

"I think it's fading," I said. "I'll phone you in the morning. Since I'm heading home anyway, I'll be in Canada in a few days."

The next day, I was in Alabama at a Day's Inn typing in *brown recluse* on the computer, and, after a bit of scrolling, found the diary of Kevin Smyth, who, two years previous in 2001, was bitten on the foot by a brown recluse spider when he was cleaning the garage. Kevin lived in a small town in Georgia. His description of the bite resembled mine. I read through a page or two of short comments, which seemed to have been written from a hospital. *Mom visited and brought some cards* was one post. Then on February 17, *Gangrene has set in and the foot has to go. Doc will do it tomorrow.* The next post was dated March 10, three weeks later. *Found out that they have to take the entire leg off.* I wanted to stop reading but could not. The next entry was dated March 31. *Guess I am not going to make it. Gangrene spreading.*

THE ART OF BURGLARY

The last entry was written by someone else. *Our beloved Kevin died April 7, 2001. Rest in Peace.*

No wonder the granddaughters went into hysterics. They weren't the only ones. As I drove north, heading for cold temperatures, I held tight to every bit of courage I could muster. Because I was in a hurry to get home, I started early and drove until late, staying in motels. At night, I sent reassuring emails to the family telling them I was still alive.

Two days later, I was driving across Illinois, my fever gone and the temperature outside close to freezing. If the spider, a tropical creature, was still hiding in the camper, it was getting the shock of its life. And once we hit Thunder Bay, Ontario, where the temperature was twenty below zero, it did not have a chance.

"Die, you bastard," I muttered. The Canadian flag was flapping in the distance, wrapping its colours around me.

Home.

214

ABOUT THE AUTHOR

Joan M. Baril

Joan M. Baril, a native of Thunder Bay, Ontario, is a short story writer with ninety pieces published mainly in Canadian literary magazines including Prairie Fire, Room, The Antigonish Review, Canadian Forum, Herizons, Ten Stories High, The New Orphic Review. Joan has won many awards for her stories and was nominated for the Journey Prize by The Antigonish Review. She has lead an active literary life including a long running blog, Literary Thunder Bay, and several newspaper columns, including "The Northern Gardener". The Northwestern Ontario Writer's Workshop awarded her the Khoui Award for "Outstanding contribution to the literature of Northwestern Ontario." The federal government awarded her with a citation for her columns on immigrant issues.

Joan loves the north. A skilled white water canoeist, she tackled many challenging rivers from the Nahanni to the Rio Grande. She also guided several canoe trips. In her small truck camper, she covered the continent, chasing her bird watching hobby, hiking, canoeing and attending literary and birding events. Later, she introduced her grandchildren to Quetico canoeing, camping and fishing. Said the youngest, "we love 'ploring and having 'ventures."

Manufactured by Amazon.ca
Bolton, ON

39093060R00132